Catnaps and Clues – A Norwegian Forest Cat Café Cozy Mystery – Book 7

by

Jinty James

Catnaps and Clues – A Norwegian Forest Cat Café Cozy Mystery – Book 7

by

Jinty James

Copyright © 2020 by Jinty James

All rights reserved

No part of this publication may be copied, reproduced in any format, by any means, electronic or otherwise, without prior consent from the copyright owner and publisher of this book.

This is a work of fiction. All characters, names, places and events are the product of the author's imagination or used fictitiously.

ISBN:9798646720147

DEDICATION

For Annie and AJ

CHAPTER 1

Lauren Crenshaw snuck a peek at her boyfriend, Detective Mitch Denman. His large tanned hands expertly steered the car down the country road towards Zeke's Ridge, a small town in Northern California. Big pine trees lined each side of the highway and in the distance, mountain peaks beckoned.

Lauren still couldn't believe that she of all people had won a prize – let alone a romantic two-night getaway at a brand-new bed and breakfast.

She was more at home making lattes and baking cupcakes in the café she ran with Annie, her Norwegian Forest Cat, a large, fluffy silver-gray tabby, and her cousin Zoe, now twenty-six and a real livewire.

Zoe had also entered the competition – in fact, she'd entered for both of them. But she'd been nothing but happy when Lauren had received the phone call that she had won second prize, two nights in the Queen suite at Flower Ridge Bed and Breakfast.

"Not long now." Mitch spoke, sending her a reassuring glance.

Lauren's heart fluttered. They'd been dating for a year now, and things had become serious. But so far this was their first romantic *overnight* getaway.

Lauren ran the café four and a half days per week, and Mitch sometimes worked overtime. However, he'd managed to have Monday off, and since the café was closed on that day, it seemed the perfect time to get away from the small town of Gold Leaf Valley, which was only around twenty minutes from their destination. It was a break for both of them, even if it was close to home.

"I wonder what the B&B will be like," Lauren mused.

"It looked good in the brochure you showed me," Mitch replied.

Zoe had waved the competition leaflets at her one day, and they'd both admired the dreamy photos of queen beds and light, airy furnishings.

"I think we're about to find out." Lauren's pulse quickened as a wooden sign stating *Flower Ridge Bed and Breakfast* came into sight.

Mitch turned onto the gravel driveway. They wound past more pine trees, large green bushes, and the occasional clump of cheery yellow buttercups bathing in the late July sun.

"It looks like this place might date from the Gold Rush era, too," Lauren commented as Mitch pulled up near the porch of the big old Victorian. Neatly painted in cream with pale blue contrast, the imposing house had pretty gingerbread trim and a small turret on the top story.

Her own modest cottage she'd inherited from her grandmother reflected that time in history, as did a lot of the houses in Gold Leaf Valley.

"Maybe someone struck it rich out here," Mitch said.

"Welcome, welcome!" A tall, big-boned woman in her mid-sixties wearing a crisp, olive dress hurried down the three white, wooden steps to greet them as they got out of the car.

"Hi! I'm Lauren Crenshaw."

"One of my competition winners." The woman beamed at her. "And this is …?" She took Mitch's hand and coyly looked at his tall, muscular frame.

"Mitch Denman." Mitch stuck out his hand.

"My boyfriend." Lauren wished her cheeks weren't flaming right now.

"How lovely! I'm Edna Lofty, proprietor of the Flower Ridge Bed and Breakfast. I have the Queen suite all ready for you. Come in out of this heat."

"Hello, folks." A tall, trim man around Edna's age trotted down the porch stairs. "I'm Harry, Edna's husband. It's a pleasure to have you here."

Lauren liked him immediately. His gray hair was neatly combed back from his forehead and he wore beige Bermuda shorts and a short-sleeved olive shirt, as if he and his wife had color-coordinated.

Edna ushered them inside the house. The foyer was directly to the right and was decorated in shades of cream, the darkest color a very pale gold. An antique style sofa with big plump cushions beckoned guests to sit down and relax. Gold velvet drapes hung at the windows.

A wooden mantel decorated with two silver candlesticks caught Lauren's gaze. A large chandelier hung from the center of the ceiling, completing the ornate, Victorian era look.

"The first prize winner will be in the King suite," Edna informed them. "Your suites are opposite each other upstairs – isn't that cozy?"

Lauren nodded, not sure what to say.

"Not too cozy, I hope," Mitch murmured in her ear.

"Now, I have our guest register for you to fill in." Edna walked behind the long mahogany counter on one side of the room and presented a brown leather book with a flourish. "You will be our very first guest to sign their name in here."

"This hasn't been a B&B for long?" Mitch guessed.

"That's right," Harry replied with a smile.

"I've wanted to run a bed and breakfast for years, haven't I, Harry?" Edna said. "And finally, we did it! Took our retirement savings – I was a substitute teacher and Harry was a mailman – sold our house in Sacramento, and here we are! I was inspired to call it Flower Ridge after Zeke's Ridge." She beamed proudly.

"Was this house a B & B before?" Lauren asked, as she wrote down her name on the first crisp white page in the book.

"No," Edna replied. "Apparently, this place has been handed down from one generation to the next, until the last heir sold it to us."

"What happened to him?" Mitch asked.

"He said the upkeep was too much for him and he was going into assisted living," Edna replied.

"It took a bit of work to get her spick and span again," Harry added, "But now she's a beauty."

"Indeed she is." Mitch glanced around the foyer.

Lauren handed the book back to Edna, who offered it to Mitch. "Your turn, Mr. Denman," she said coyly.

Mitch raised his eyebrow, but complied.

"I don't think it's really necessary for both of them to fill in their details," Harry protested mildly.

"We must do things properly." Edna tutted.

"Let me show you your room," Harry offered. "Do you need help with your bags?"

"No, we're good." Mitch smiled briefly, picking up both their weekend bags.

"It's a suite, Harry," Edna corrected him.

"Sorry, dear."

"Well, now, I'll show you the Queen *suite*." Edna took the lead up the staircase, the mahogany polished to a gleaming shine.

Lauren followed Edna, while Harry brought up the rear.

Were all B&B owners as quirky as Edna seemed to be?

"Here we are." Edna unlocked a wooden door with a lavender plaque in the center and urged them inside.

"It's beautiful." Lauren's eyes widened as she took in the large bed with an ivory and gold coverlet and plenty of plump pillows, just like in the leaflet. The walls were painted a matching ivory, and there was a small chandelier hanging from the ceiling. She looked down at the carpet – a beige-gold shade. A bowl of lavender pot-pourri scented the air, perched on a small bedside table next to a silver candlestick.

"There's another bedroom through here." Edna opened a connecting door with a flourish. A large bed, made up the same way as the first one, dominated the small space.

"The bathroom is over here." Harry gestured to a discreet door near the second bedroom.

Lauren couldn't resist; she peeked inside. A gleaming claw-footed bathtub, walk-in shower, and a double vanity, along with a small wall mirror.

"No expense spared," Edna said with satisfaction.

"I can see that," Lauren said softly. She didn't think she'd stayed anywhere as nice as this before.

"Well now, I guess we'll leave you two love-birds alone." Edna nodded.

"Remember, there are *two* beds in your suite."

"We'll remember," Mitch said dryly.

"Let us know if you need anything," Harry told them.

"We'll be downstairs. At *all* times." After a beat, Edna added, "Our bedroom is down there."

Harry gave them a friendly smile as he and his wife left the room.

"Wow." Mitch waited until the door shut behind the couple.

"Mm-hm." Lauren sank down on the bed. Plush and comfy.

"I thought it sounded too good to be true."

"What?" Lauren frowned. "Me winning this weekend away?"

"Harry seems nice enough, but Edna …" He shook his head. "I bet she'll pop in a few times to see if we need anything."

"Maybe she's just enthusiastic," Lauren offered. "We *are* her first guests. She probably doesn't want anything to go wrong."

"And I'm sure nothing will," Mitch reassured her. He pulled out his phone from his pants' pocket and showed it to her. "I've switched my phone off. How about you?"

With a guilty start, Lauren dug into her purse and retrieved her phone. "Good idea." She'd left it turned on during the drive in case Zoe wanted to contact her. Her cousin was cat sitting Annie this weekend, or was Annie Zoe sitting?

Her phone buzzed just as her finger hovered on the off switch.

"Zoe," Mitch guessed.

"Hi, Lauren." Zoe's voice bubbled from the phone. "Are you there yet? What does the room look like?" She added, "Annie wanted me to call you."

"Brrt!" Annie added from the other end.

"I think we should use the video app," Zoe said. A second later, Zoe and Annie appeared on the phone screen.

"Hi." Lauren smiled at the two of them.

Zoe's brunette pixie cut highlighted her cute features and sparkling brown eyes, while Annie peered through the screen, her green eyes wide with curiosity. Her silver-gray fur was thick and luxurious.

"What does the room look like?" Zoe asked. "Hi, Mitch," she added, giving him a little wave.

"Brrt," Annie called.

"Hi, Annie. Hi, Zoe." Mitch's lips quirked up.

"The room is beautiful," Lauren told them. "Look, here's the bed."

"Ooh, just like the leaflet, Annie," Zoe told the feline.

"Brrp."

Lauren moved slowly around the room with the phone, showing the duo the furnishings. When she finished the tour, she noticed Mitch relaxing in the gold brocade wing chair near the bed.

"So what are you two going to be doing tonight?" Lauren asked as she halted near Mitch's chair.

"Chris is coming over and we're going to order pizza." Zoe grinned. "And Annie will have chicken in gravy."

"Brrt!" Annie sounded pleased about her dinner menu.

"What are you two going to be doing?" Zoe waggled her eyebrows, making her look like a mischievous elf.

"Zoe!" Lauren hoped Mitch hadn't heard her cousin's question.

"Having a relaxing weekend." Mitch spoke.

"Then we'll leave you to it," Zoe promised. "Won't we, Annie?"

"Brrt!"

Lauren waved goodbye to them, waiting until Zoe ended the call before she turned off the phone. She'd never been away overnight from Annie before. She knew Zoe would take good care of her, but …

"I'm sure Annie will be fine." Mitch stood and wrapped his arms around her.

"Thanks." She snuggled into his broad, muscular chest. Everything felt so right when she was in his arms.

"Knock, knock." Edna opened the door. "I thought you two might like some fresh towels."

Startled, Lauren stepped out of Mitch's embrace. "I thought there were towels already in the bathroom," she said, flustered.

"You can never have too many." Edna beamed over the mound of fluffy white towels she held against her chest, her eyes sharp.

"Thanks." Mitch took them from her.

"Anything else you need?" Edna glanced around the room, her gaze lingering on the untouched bed. "More pillows? More pot-pourri? More—"

"I'm sure they have everything they need." Harry appeared in the doorway. "Sorry to bother you folks."

"It's fine," Lauren replied, not sure what else to say.

Mitch nodded at the older man.

"Come on, Edna." Harry took his wife's arm.

"Let me know if you need anything. Anything at all," she told them as her husband escorted her from the room. "Oh, and what time you'd like breakfast. I've had breakfast menus printed, and they're downstairs. I'll just run down and get them and be back in a jiffy!"

"You can do that later," Harry told her gently as he shut the door behind them.

"Phew." Mitch sank down on the bed. "What did I tell you?"

"Mmm." Lauren hated to think he was right. Would Edna interrupt them again? She glanced at the door.

Mitch must have read her thoughts because he strode over to it and shot the bolt home.

"There," he said in satisfaction. "If Edna has any more towels for us, she'll have to wait until we let her in. *If* we let her in."

Locked in a room with Mitch. A shiver of anticipation danced down her spine. She hadn't decided yet whether they should use two beds or one this weekend. Mitch had told her when she'd invited him for the weekend that the decision was up to her and they wouldn't do anything she wasn't comfortable with. Which made her fall for him even harder.

She touched the gold L necklace he'd given her in January, the metal smooth against her fingertips. She'd barely taken it off since.

"I wonder how long they've been married?" Lauren pondered.

"Edna and Harry?"

She nodded.

"Maybe too long for Harry."

"Mitch!"

"But that wouldn't happen to us," he told her decisively.

"It wouldn't?" Her heart gave a little trip.

"I can't see you being nosy and bossing me around."

"I hope that doesn't mean you would be nosy and bossing me around – and Annie," she added. Just to doublecheck that he knew that she and Annie were a package deal.

"I wouldn't." He chuckled. "I don't think Annie would let me, anyway. Zoe and Chris on the other hand …"

Lauren grabbed a pillow and threw it at him. He tossed it back gently. She threw it again. This could get interesting—

Rap. Rap. Rap.

Mitch groaned.

"Should we?" Lauren whispered.

"No." He shook his head.

"Yoo hoo," Edna called through the closed door. "I've got your breakfast menus here, just like I promised. If you let me in, I can explain each dish."

Rap. Rap. Rap.

"I can come back later if you two are … busy." The last word sounded disapproving. "Shouldn't you be out for a walk on such a beautiful afternoon? It's not quite as warm outside now. We have a large garden for our guests to enjoy. Why don't I show it to you?"

It was too much. Lauren clapped a hand over her mouth to stifle her giggle.

"I think she deserves a medal for persistence." Mitch chuckled reluctantly before striding over and unlocking the door.

"Oh, there you are!" Edna straightened up and smiled at Mitch.

Lauren's eyes widened. Had Edna been spying on them through the keyhole?

"What can we do for you?" Mitch kept his tone pleasant.

"Breakfast menus!" Edna thrust two laminated cards at him. "I'm happy to explain each dish to you. Now, what time would you like your breakfast?"

Mitch cocked an eyebrow in Lauren's direction.

"Umm, we haven't really thought about that yet," she offered.

"Why don't we let you know this evening?" Mitch suggested.

"Of course, of course," Edna replied. "Now where are you two going to dinner tonight? I'm happy to recommend a few restaurants in Zeke's Ridge. If you tell them Edna sent you, I'm sure you'll get the best table there!"

"Really?" Lauren asked. To her knowledge there were only three in the small town, and she and Mitch had often dined at the Italian one.

"Oh, yes," Edna said earnestly. "When we moved here I visited each restaurant and told them I would recommend them to my guests if they gave them special treatment."

"How did that go?" Mitch asked.

"They said they'd be happy to," Edna replied. "No problem, they said. Now, I think the best place for you two to visit tonight is the nice Italian restaurant here."

"Why is that?" Mitch asked.

"Because they have wonderful lasagna and risotto, as well as pasta dishes. Harry and I dined there when we first moved here and we were both impressed with the food."

"We'll keep it in mind," Mitch told her.

"Good, good." Edna hovered in the doorway. "Now, what else can I tell you about the property? You really should see the garden, there's buttercups and lilacs and daisies in bloom—"

"Edna." Harry appeared behind her. "We've talked about this."

"I'm just delivering the breakfast menus," Edna told him innocently. "You know what they say, breakfast is the most important meal of the day."

"I think I just heard a car pull up," Harry told her.

"Really?" Edna turned. "Maybe it's our first prize winner! I'll go check." She hurried down the staircase, her shoes tapping on the wooden boards.

"I'm sorry about this," Harry told them. "I think my wife is excited about having her first guests this weekend."

"It's understandable," Lauren replied.

"No problem," Mitch said politely.

With a nod, Harry left them. Mitch bolted the door – again.

"I didn't hear a car – did you?" Lauren remarked.

"No." He shook his head, a small smile playing around his mouth. "I think Harry knows just how to handle Edna after all."

***

Lauren and Mitch *did* end up in the garden.

"It *is* beautiful," Lauren said, her hand engulfed in his as they strolled around the grounds. White daisies, lilac, and butterfly bushes attracted orange and black butterflies, their wings fluttering as they landed on the flowers.

"I guess Edna was right about one thing," Mitch replied with a smile.

After their romantic stroll, they got ready for dinner. Lauren looked longingly at the claw-footed tub, complete with an inviting jar of bath salts, but settled for a hot shower instead, the water pressure perfect. The scent of lavender mixed with the steam as she used the complimentary shower gel.

Mitch was already dressed when she emerged from the bathroom. His navy button dress shirt, black slacks, and short dark hair enhanced his good looks. A faint trace of light citrus aftershave teased her senses. He smiled when he saw her.

"Let's enjoy ourselves this evening." He held out his hand.

She returned his smile as she placed her hand in his. Tonight was going to be perfect. And to top it all off, Edna hadn't knocked on their door since she'd given them the breakfast menus.

Once they descended the staircase and entered the foyer, Edna looked up from the reception desk.

"Are you two going out for dinner?" Her tone was coy. "Don't you look nice, dear?" she said to Lauren.

"Thank you." Lauren glanced down at her plum wrap dress, one of her favorite outfits, and one she thought flattered her curves, and her light brown hair with natural hints of gold.

"I'd like you two to meet the other guests," Edna continued. "Our first prize winner. Barbara Frynell and her sister Donna. They'll be in the King suite." She gestured to the plump, cushioned sofa. Two women in their fifties looked up from their brochures.

"Hello, I'm Donna." Attractive, with discreet make-up and short, layered brown hair, she smiled at them.

"And I'm Barbara," the other woman said pleasantly. She shared some of her sister's features, but her cinnamon hair was cut into a feathered bob.

After Lauren and Mitch introduced themselves, Edna said, "I need you two ladies to sign the guest register."

"Of course." Barbara rose and walked across to the reception desk.

Edna looked expectantly at Donna. After a moment, Donna got up and joined her sister.

"It was nice meeting both of you," Mitch said politely. "Perhaps we'll see you later."

"Where are you two going for dinner?" Edna asked, switching her gaze from Donna picking up a pen to Lauren and Mitch.

"We haven't decided yet," Mitch replied.

"Don't forget my recommendation for the Italian restaurant," Edna told him.

"We won't," Mitch replied dryly.

Edna turned her attention to the sisters as Donna put down the pen. "Thank you." She picked up the book and squinted at their entries. "Hmm. It didn't click before. You both have the same surname, if I'm reading your handwriting correctly, Donna, because it is *not* very legible. If you'd been one of my students …" she tutted, then continued, "*but* you're both wearing wedding rings." Edna's sharp-eyed gaze zeroed in on first Donna's hand, and then Barbara's.

"I'm a widow," Donna replied. "I wear my wedding ring to honor my husband."

"But your last name is Frynell for both of you." Edna furrowed her brow.

"We've always used our maiden names," Donna told her. "Our mother was a modern thinker and so are we. Aren't we, Barbara?"

"Yes," Barbara replied, looking a little puzzled.

"Thank you, ladies." Edna shut the guest book with a snap. "Let me show you to your suite. I'm sure you'll love it."

Lauren and Mitch nodded goodbye and headed toward the car.

"Phew." Mitch fastened his seatbelt. "I think Edna would make a good detective."

"I think you're right," Lauren agreed.

Mitch drove into the small town of Zeke's Ridge. The weather had cooled a little but the early evening sun shone above a distant mountain.

"If the Italian place wasn't already our favorite, I think Edna recommending it would put me off trying it," Mitch admitted as he pulled up outside the wooden storefront. Red checkered drapes and sparkling clean windows invited people to step inside and satisfy their appetite.

"I know what you mean." Lauren nodded.

"So … Italian? Or would you like pizza or steak?"

"You know I love this place." Lauren smiled at him and gestured to the entrance.

They were greeted by one of the regular wait staff and shown their favorite table in the corner. The savory aroma of herbs and tomato sauce drifting out from the kitchen tempted Lauren's appetite.

"It's nice to see you again," the bubbly redhead told them as she handed them menus. Her name badge read Sam.

"We're staying at Flower Ridge Bed and Breakfast," Lauren told her, unable to resist. "I won a prize in their contest."

"That's wonderful," Sam congratulated her.

"Actually, Edna recommended this place to us. She didn't know that we've been here before," Mitch added.

"Oh – Edna." Sam quickly closed her mouth, as if aware she'd said something wrong.

"What is it?" Lauren asked curiously.

"Only – only that Edna came in here when she and her husband first moved to the area, and asked – demanded, really – that we give her guests special treatment." The girl paused. "Our manager Frank wasn't impressed."

"Oh." Lauren didn't know what else to say.

"Frank just agreed with everything she said, but was fuming after she left. He said we give all our customers special treatment and that wasn't going to change."

"Your service has always been excellent," Mitch noted.

"And the food is amazing," Lauren added.

"Thanks, guys." Sam looked pleased. "I'll make sure to let Frank know, too."

"At least I'm not the only one Edna rubs the wrong way." Mitch closed his menu with a snap.

"But our room – suite – is so beautiful." Lauren held out her hand. "And I used the lavender shower gel – it has such a nice scent – see?"

He smiled, inhaling quietly. "I noticed when we left the room." His dark brown gaze encompassed her, making Lauren feel warm all over.

"Although Edna might be rubbing people the wrong way, she seems to know what guests want in a B&B."

"I suppose." Mitch nodded. "Apart from constantly interrupting them in their room."

"Good point," she conceded.

Their entrees arrived, mushroom risotto for Lauren, and lasagna for Mitch, and as they ate, they talked about their plans for the following week, making a date for dinner on Wednesday, when they would be back in Gold Leaf Valley.

For dessert they ordered the tiramisu, a dessert that Lauren loved. She savored the textures and flavors of soft coffee-soaked ladyfingers, cream, mascarpone, and cocoa.

After coffee, Mitch paid the bill and they returned to the B&B, the night sky a dusky blue-black.

"Maybe Edna and Harry are watching a movie right now," he said optimistically as he opened her car door. "So they won't be lurking at the front door, ready to pounce on us as soon as we enter."

"You mean just Edna, don't you?" Lauren teased. "Because I don't think Harry could pounce on anyone. He seems a nice man."

"I guess we're about to find out." Mitch opened the front door.

Lauren hesitated, wondering for a second if Edna was going to greet them with a "Yoo hoo," but everything seemed quiet. The lights on the foyer chandelier were on but apart from that the place was deserted.

"Let's make a run for it." Mitch took her hand.

"Hi, folks." Harry appeared from a discreet inner door at one end of the foyer.

Lauren started, her heart racing at the surprise appearance.

"Hi," Mitch said, giving her hand a reassuring squeeze.

"Have you seen Edna?" Harry asked them. "She was going to check on something, but that was a while ago."

"No, we've just come back from dinner," Mitch informed him.

"Oh, of course. Sorry to disturb you." Harry smiled. "Don't mind me – I'm sure Edna will appear at any second."

A scream echoed through the house. And another.

Lauren's eyes widened.

"It seems to be coming from up there." Mitch looked at the mahogany staircase with narrowed eyes.

"And it doesn't sound like Edna." Harry started up the stairs.

CHAPTER 2

"Stay behind us," Mitch tossed over his shoulder to Lauren, as he overtook Harry on the stairs.

She didn't think that would be a problem. The scream had sounded terrified and she didn't want to be first on the scene, but she didn't want to be left alone down in the foyer, either.

Lauren raced up the stairs behind Harry.

"There!" Donna pointed to the end of the hall with a shaking finger.

A figure lay crumpled on the floor.

"What's happened?" Donna's sister asked her, coming out of their suite.

"I – I don't know," Donna sobbed. "I heard a noise and came out to see what it was, and I saw Edna lying there!"

"Edna?" Harry sped past Mitch to the female on the floor. "No, not Edna!"

"Let me see." Mitch joined him. "I'm a detective."

Lauren bit her lip, watching Mitch check for a pulse.

He gravely shook his head. "I'm sorry." He placed a hand on Harry's shoulder.

"No." A tear rolled down Harry's lined face. "It can't be. She was so excited to be opening this place. Said it was her lifelong dream to run a bed and breakfast. She thought having this contest would help put us on the map."

Mitch helped Harry to his feet.

"I'm sorry," Lauren said awkwardly.

"I have to call this in." Mitch pulled out his cell phone, then looked at Lauren. "I need you to take everyone downstairs to the foyer. I'll be there in a moment."

Lauren nodded, hearing Mitch explain their situation on his cell.

"I can't believe this." Barbara looked around wildly. "Who could have done it?"

"I don't know," Harry said brokenly, following Lauren down the stairs. "Edna didn't have an enemy in the world. She was so full of vim and vigor. What am I going to do without her?"

Lauren's heart went out to him. What would her reaction be if that was Mitch or Zoe or Annie lying there on the hall floor? But it wasn't, she told herself. Thank goodness.

They all sat down in the foyer and looked at each other. Mitch hurried down the stairs.

"The police will be here soon. Detective Castern as well."

Lauren groaned inwardly. The officer had been in charge of the last murder in Gold Leaf Valley and had seemed keen to solve it quickly. She just hoped he didn't think she or Mitch were suspects in Edna's death.

"How—" Donna cleared her throat. "How did she – Edna – die?"

"It looks like blunt force trauma to the head," Mitch replied. "But we won't know for sure until the medical examiner completes his report."

"Why?" Harry looked up at Mitch, who stood while everyone else sat down on the antique sofas. "Why would someone kill my Edna?"

"I don't know," Mitch said gently. "Has she had disagreements with anyone recently?"

"No." Harry shook his head. "We've been so busy here, sprucing the place up, we haven't had much contact with people, except when we've gone into Zeke's Ridge to get supplies."

"Ah." Mitch nodded.

"What does that mean?" Barbara asked eagerly.

"Just that," Mitch replied. "When Detective Castern arrives, he'll probably take everyone's statement."

"Then what will happen?" Donna asked, her eyes wide.

"I'm not sure," Mitch told her. "We'll have to wait and see."

Lauren knew that Mitch had run plenty of investigations, and had been involved in solving murders as well. She was certain he knew what would happen next. Maybe he didn't want to second guess Detective Castern's investigative methods or share too much information with potential suspects.

"Maybe we should have something to drink," Lauren offered hesitantly. "Like a—"

"Good idea." Barbara rose and crossed to the wooden antique hutch where a crystal decanter with matching snifters resided. "My nerves definitely need to be settled."

"I meant a cup of hot tea – or hot chocolate," Lauren protested. "With plenty of sugar." She knew that sugar could help with the shock of stumbling across a murder victim.

The splash of the golden cognac into the snifter seemed to catch their attention as Barbara poured herself a stiff drink.

"That was Edna's idea," Harry mourned. "She thought it would add real class to have some expensive brandy down here and offer it to the guests."

"Harry?" Barbara tilted the heavy looking decanter in his direction. "Want one?"

"I think Lauren's idea of a hot chocolate might be better," Mitch said. "We can all go into the kitchen together while we wait for law enforcement."

"But *you're* law enforcement," Donna pointed out.

"And my job is to keep you all together," he told her.

"What do you do, Lauren?" Donna enquired.

"I run a café with my cousin in Gold Leaf Valley," she replied. "And with Annie, my cat." The thought of her fluffy silver tabby brought a tiny smile to her face.

The sound of a vehicle pulling up outside a few seconds later brought Lauren a measure of relief. She trusted Mitch to do his job well but reinforcements couldn't be a bad thing, could they?

Detective Castern strode into the foyer, flanked by two uniformed officers. After a quick conversation with Mitch in low tones, the middle-aged man hurried up the staircase, one officer following him. The other officer stayed behind in the foyer.

"What's going to happen?" Lauren asked Mitch.

"Castern will question us all once he's seen the vic – Edna," he murmured.

Barbara swallowed the rest of her drink in a big gulp. "Excellent cognac," she pronounced.

"Barbara, please." Donna nudged her.

"Harry should have some." Barbara poured some into another glass and held it out to him.

"Thanks," he replied wanly, and took a sip.

Barbara made to pour some more for herself, but Mitch stopped her.

"I don't think that's a good idea," he told her.

"He's right," Donna chimed in. "Come and sit down next to me." She put an arm around her sister and guided her to the sofa.

"What is my husband going to say about this?" Barbara sniffed. "The first chance we have to get away and have some time to ourselves and this – this happens!"

Detective Castern came down the stairs. "I'll see you one at a time," he informed them. "Starting with you, Denman." He looked at Mitch.

The officer who had gone up stairs with Detective Castern seemed to have remained up there. Probably guarding the scene, Lauren thought.

Detective Castern and Mitch went outside on the porch, closing the door behind them. A few minutes later, Mitch returned, his mouth set in a firm line.

"Your turn," he murmured to Lauren, gesturing to the front door.

Lauren walked slowly outside. She didn't know what she could tell the detective. With a feeling of relief, she realized she and Mitch were each other's alibi. Surely the detective would only take a brief statement from her, especially since he worked with Mitch?

Detective Castern did not seem pleased to see her. He quizzed her about winning the second prize of two nights in the Queen suite, and exactly what her and Mitch's movements had been since they had left Gold Leaf Valley that afternoon.

He seemed especially interested in what time they had gone out to dinner, and if Edna had still been alive then.

"Of course she was," Lauren protested. "We were all in the foyer – apart from Harry. Mitch, me, Donna, and Barbara. That was just before seven-thirty." She felt guilty for mentioning Harry's absence at that time, but she didn't want to lie or leave anything out.

After jotting down the details of the restaurant she and Mitch had visited, he finally told her she could go. Mitch would take her home to Gold Leaf Valley.

"You might as well forget about staying here this weekend," he told her. "This place is going to be closed until further notice."

Poor Harry. Lauren's knees wobbled as she walked back into the house.

"Are you okay?" Mitch asked, scanning her expression.

She nodded. "Detective Castern said we can go home now."

"Yeah."

"What about our things in our room?"

"Have they found the murder weapon yet?" Barbara's question broke into their conversation.

"You'll have to ask Detective Castern that," Mitch replied. He held out his hand to Lauren. "Let's see if we can grab our stuff."

She followed him up the staircase, averting her eyes as she reached the top. She did not want to see Edna lying on the floor.

The officer stood guard near the murder scene.

"Is it okay to get our bags from our room?" Mitch asked him. "Castern said we could go home."

"Yes, I guess so." The officer scratched his head. "He hasn't told me you can't, and besides, you're one of us."

"Thanks." Mitch gave him a brief smile, then ushered Lauren into the room.

She packed her weekend bag, then scanned the room to make sure she hadn't forgotten anything.

"All set?" Mitch asked, zipping shut his bag.

"Yes," she replied, sadly looking around the posh bedroom – no, suite. That's what Edna had called it.

"Everything's going to be okay," he reassured her.

"Not for Harry."

"No. Not for Harry." There was regret in his voice.

CHAPTER 3

"OMG!" Zoe's eyes widened as Lauren filled her in on what had happened at the B&B. They sat in the living room of the cottage that Lauren, Annie, and Zoe called home.

"Brrt!" Annie echoed, sitting up straight and tall on Lauren's lap. Mitch sat beside her on the blue sofa, while Zoe sat on Lauren's other side, and Chris, a friend of Mitch's and now Zoe's boyfriend, sat opposite, in an armchair.

Lauren gently stroked Annie's soft, silver-gray fur, the motion soothing her.

"I wonder why someone killed her," Zoe's brown eyes were alive with curiosity. "Maybe she barged into the wrong room too many times and saw something she shouldn't have."

"That's a possibility," Mitch replied. "But there were only two other guests besides us."

"Sisters," Lauren added.

"Hmm." Zoe steepled her fingertips together like a modern Sherlock Holmes.

"Did they find the weapon?" Chris asked, interest flickering across his even, attractive features.

"Not yet," Mitch said. "All I know is, it was something heavy enough to kill."

They were silent for a moment.

"Maybe we shouldn't talk about this anymore at the moment," Lauren suggested, glancing down at Annie, still sitting in her lap, her feline ears pricked.

"Oh, yeah." Zoe nodded.

"You must be tired." Mitch wrapped his arm around Lauren. "I'll say goodnight."

"Me too." Chris rose.

Zoe looked disappointed, but followed Chris out to the front door.

"Do you want to do anything tomorrow?" Mitch asked her. "I've still got the next two days off, unless I'm called into the office now they know I'm back."

"I'd like that." She smiled at him.

"Brrt," Annie agreed. She reached out and gently touched his arm.

"Do you want to come over here? I think Annie wants you to."

"Why not?" His lips tilted into a smile.

***

The next day, Mitch came over for lunch with Lauren and Annie. Zoe had borrowed Lauren's car to visit Chris in Sacramento, one hour away. He was due at work that afternoon for his shift as a paramedic, but they'd already made plans to meet up for lunch first.

If there hadn't been a murder the night before, Lauren would have totally enjoyed herself. But she couldn't help thinking about poor Edna lying on the hall floor. Who could have hated her enough to kill her? Or …

"Do you think it was an accident?" she suddenly asked as Mitch sipped his coffee. They'd just finished lunch.

"Brrt?" Annie added. She sat next to Lauren at the kitchen table, while Mitch sat opposite them.

"One heck of an accident if it was," he replied.

"What if Edna stumbled and hit her head on something?" Lauren pursued.

"Maybe," he conceded, "but what could it have been? It would have to be in that hallway. I doubt she would have been able to climb the stairs after banging her head that hard."

Lauren thought back to their room – no, suite – at the B&B. Their floor had seemed to consist of only the two guest suites. No furniture or hooks dangling from the walls. Surely the old-fashioned door knobs wouldn't have inflicted a fatal injury?

"Why don't we talk about something else?" Mitch suggested.

"Like what?" She attempted a smile.

"My parents would like to meet you one day."

"They would?" She stared at him.

"Brrt?" Annie also stared at him, her green eyes wide.

"Yeah." He smiled.

Mitch didn't talk about his parents much – when Lauren had first met him, he'd seemed quite guarded, but had gradually opened up over the last year. She didn't think he gave his heart lightly.

"They're driving around the country in an RV," he added. "They have a home base in San Diego, and said when they return home, they'd love to meet you –

they did threaten to stop by the café and say hi to you on their way home."

Gulp.

"Okay," she replied softly. She wondered what his parents were like – would his dad be just like him? What about his mother?

"They'll like you," he reassured her.

She hadn't introduced Mitch to her parents yet – she hadn't been sure when to suggest it.

"I hope so."

"Brrt." *Me too.*

"I'm sure my mom will like you, Annie," he told her, "although she's never had a cat." He'd told Lauren a while ago that he'd never had much to do with cats and at first hadn't known how to interact with Annie. Lately though, he'd seemed a lot more comfortable around the Norwegian Forest Cat.

"Brrp." Annie sounded as if she understood.

After lunch they took a walk around the neighborhood. Annie joined them, wearing her harness, with Lauren holding the lead. Then finally, Mitch kissed her goodbye when they returned to the cottage. Zoe had returned too, Lauren's car parked outside on the street, gleaming like new.

"It looks like Zoe had your car washed," Mitch observed.

"That was nice of her." Lauren didn't mind lending her car to Zoe whenever she needed it, and Zoe paid her back by paying for gas or doing something thoughtful like this.

As if she knew they were talking about her, Zoe suddenly appeared on the front porch.

"Hey, Lauren, I think we should visit Mrs. Finch tomorrow and tell her about the murder!"

"Brrt!"

CHAPTER 4

So much for Lauren's dreamy weekend, although spending Sunday with Mitch had been romantic in its own way.

The next morning after breakfast, Zoe commandeered her and Annie.

"First we'll visit Mrs. Finch, and then we'll go to the grocery store in case we need anything."

"But we did extra shopping on Friday," Lauren protested. Usually they visited the small supermarket on Mondays when the café was closed but because Lauren had planned to be away until Monday afternoon, they'd bought extra supplies the previous week.

"I know, but what if you suddenly come up with a brand-new cupcake idea?" Zoe's brown eyes sparkled. "You'd need all the ingredients to experiment."

"Brrt!"

Annie had helped Lauren in the past with mixing up new cupcake flavors in the cottage kitchen and seemed to enjoy her role as 'supervisor', while Zoe relished tasting each new creation.

Since the weather was fine, although a little warm, they decided to walk around the block to Mrs. Finch's house. As they approached the sweet, cream Victorian, with the neat lawn and pink Dahlias, Lauren didn't like the fact they were going to mention another death in the community, albeit one twenty minutes away.

"I wonder if Mrs. Finch knew Edna," Zoe mused as she knocked on the front door.

"Good point." The elderly lady had lived in Gold Leaf Valley for many years and knew a lot of the locals.

"Brrt," Annie agreed.

"Hello, dears." Mrs. Finch opened the door and beamed, the orange dots of rouge on her cheeks looking like the California poppies that had bloomed in her garden earlier that summer. "Lauren, I thought you were staying at the bed and breakfast this weekend."

"She was," Zoe replied dramatically. "And then there was a murder!"

"Not another one." Mrs. Finch sounded shocked. "Oh dear, where are my manners? Come in, come in."

They followed her down the lilac painted hall to the living room, decorated in tones of fawn and beige.

"Sit down," Mrs. Finch urged, sinking into an armchair.

Annie hopped up on the sofa next to Lauren, then jumped down and ran across to the senior, elegantly leaping onto the upholstered arm of the chair.

"Hello, Annie, dear." Mrs. Finch beamed as she gently stroked the silver-gray tabby. Lauren knew she was one of Annie's favorite humans, besides herself and Zoe.

Zoe launched into Lauren's adventure on the weekend, Lauren occasionally adding her own observations. When they had finished, Mrs. Finch shook her head.

"My goodness," she exclaimed. "The poor woman – and her husband."

"Do you know them, Mrs. Finch?" Zoe asked eagerly.

"No, I'm afraid I don't," she replied. "You say they're from Sacramento originally."

"That's what Edna told us when we arrived," Lauren commented.

"I'm afraid their names don't ring a bell," Mrs. Finch answered regretfully.

Zoe then talked about her current pottery efforts. In the last year she'd tried knitting, crochet, string-art, bead jewelry, and had now settled on pottery for the past few months.

"I can't wait until you see the mugs I've made." Zoe beamed. "I've painted Annie's picture on them and also the name of the café. I'm going to sell them to our customers!"

"They're going to be displayed on the counter," Lauren added, hoping her cousin wouldn't be disappointed if a flurry of sales didn't happen right away.

"You must let me buy one," Mrs. Finch told her.

"Awesome!" Zoe grinned. "I'll put one away for you in case they all sell out tomorrow!"

"Zoe's done a good job of capturing Annie's likeness," Lauren added. She couldn't draw or paint, and hadn't realized that Zoe had talent in that area.

"But the mugs themselves are a *tiny* bit wobbly." Zoe made a moue.

"I'm sure they look very good," Mrs. Finch said encouragingly.

"We'll see." But Zoe seemed cheered by the comment.

After making Mrs. Finch a cup of coffee using her pod machine, they said goodbye to her, Zoe promising again to put away one of the pottery mugs for her.

"Just think." Zoe's eyes sparkled as they left Mrs. Finch's house. "By this time tomorrow, my mugs might have sold out already!"

***

Except they didn't. At lunchtime on Tuesday, Zoe hadn't sold a single cup – apart from the one she'd earmarked for Mrs. Finch.

"I think it's my best one," she told Lauren earnestly, taking it out from behind the counter. "See, hardly any wobbles—" she pointed to a slight bulge on one side of the cup "—and the handle is pretty comfy to hold. Look!" She slid three fingers into and around the handle.

"The handle makes it easy to lift it up and bring it to your mouth so you can enjoy your coffee or tea or whatever you want to drink."

The mug was a decent size. Zoe had painted them white, with Annie's face appearing on one side, and the words *Norwegian Forest Cat Café* appearing on the other side, although some of the letters in the word *Norwegian* were a *tiny* bit squished.

Not that Annie had seemed to mind. When Zoe had shown her the mugs with her likeness on them, she'd brrted with pleasure.

"Maybe you should save one for Annie," Lauren suggested. "You know how she likes to drink out of my cup sometimes when I've got lukewarm water."

"I already have." Zoe grinned. "Three. One for each of us."

"Thanks." Lauren smiled at her cousin. It was hard to imagine life before Zoe came for a visit one weekend and they'd all decided – Annie too – that she should stay and work in the café with them and become their roomie. It certainly hadn't been dull, that's for sure.

"I wonder where Mrs. Finch is?" Zoe asked, putting the mug away behind the counter. "She usually comes in the morning."

"I hope she's okay." Lauren frowned. "We could check on her after we close this afternoon."

"Deal." Zoe nodded.

So far none of their regulars had stopped by, but the morning had seen a steady stream of customers arriving for cupcakes, Danishes, lattes, and cappuccinos.

Although Lauren baked the cupcakes, her baker Ed created the Danishes the café was renowned for. Big, burly, and gruff, he had monster rolling pins for arms but his pastries were light, flaky, and totally delicious.

"Hi, girls." Their friend Martha suddenly barreled into the café, pushing her rolling walker.

"Brrt!" Annie jumped down from her pink cat bed and ran to the *Please Wait to be Seated* sign to greet her.

"Hi, cutie pie." Martha beamed down at her. With her curly gray hair and determination, the senior was a force to reckon with. "Where should I sit today?"

Annie determined where each customer sat, leading them to a table she chose for them. Sometimes she joined them, especially if they were her favorites, and other times she seemed to know when someone preferred to be on their own.

"Brrt!" Annie leaped onto the padded vinyl seat of the walker. "Brrt!" *This way.*

When Martha reached a table for four near the counter, Annie chirped, "Brrp." *Here.*

"Good choice," Martha complimented, sinking down into a chair.

Annie hopped off the walker and onto one of the matching pine chairs at the table.

"Hi, Martha." Lauren approached. "What can we get you?"

"How was your weekend away?" Martha winked at her. "Your *romantic* weekend away?"

Lauren's cheeks burned.

"I wish I'd won that contest," Martha continued, not seeming to notice Lauren's discomfort, "but I don't have anyone I could take. Not in a *boyfriend* way."

"It didn't go exactly according to plan," Lauren admitted.

"Why not?" Martha's eyes rounded. "Mitch did go with you, didn't he? He didn't get called into work at the last moment?"

"No, but—" Lauren hesitated. No doubt the events of Saturday night were all over Zeke's Ridge by now, and before long, all over Gold Leaf Valley as well. Besides, she and Zoe had already told Mrs. Finch.

"Edna was murdered," she said in a low rush.

"Who?" Martha frowned.

"The lady running the bed and breakfast."

"No!" Martha's mouth formed an O. "When was that? Saturday? Sunday? Monday?"

Lauren quickly told her the bare facts, then took her order of a large hot chocolate even though it was summer, and a cinnamon crumble cupcake. She fled to the counter to start the order.

"I guess you told Martha," Zoe said, plating the cupcake.

"Uh-huh," Lauren replied, concentrating on foaming the milk.

"Sorry. I could have told her." Zoe patted Lauren on the shoulder. "Ooh, I know, I'll distract her by showing Annie's mugs."

"Good idea." Lauren nodded.

She watched Zoe hurry over to Martha's table, her tray containing the cupcake and a pottery mug.

"Look what I've made, Martha," she heard her cousin say as she showed her Annie's portrait on the cup.

"Look at that!" Martha exclaimed, holding out the mug and then looking at Annie. "I've got to have one! It looks just like you, Annie."

"Brrt!" Annie seemed to agree.

Lauren smiled to herself. Zoe was a good wing woman.

Zoe beamed as Lauren brought over Martha's beverage. "Now I've sold two mugs!"

"Wait 'til I tell them down at the senior center about your pottery project." Martha stirred her hot chocolate, crammed with pink and white marshmallows, then took a big sip. "They'll all want one."

"I hope so." Zoe looked delighted.

They chatted to Martha for a few minutes, then more customers trickled in.

"Maybe I should start making extra mugs," Zoe said enthusiastically as she plated apricot Danishes and vanilla cupcakes. "So I have a steady supply for customers."

"When do you have another pottery class?" Lauren asked.

"Next week. What if I sell out before then?"

"Write down the names of everyone who wanted one and missed out, and take a deposit," Lauren suggested, not wanting her cousin to be disappointed if sales weren't as brisk as she hoped.

"Good idea!"

The rest of the day passed quickly. Mrs. Finch visited that afternoon and admired the mug Zoe had set aside for her, telling Annie she would use it that evening.

"Let's start closing up," Zoe suggested, just before five o'clock. They were the only ones in the café.

"I'll do the dishes," Lauren said.

Ed had already gone for the day; he started early and finished early. He'd also left the kitchen gleaming after he'd departed so there weren't many plates and cups to wash.

Lauren had a commercial dishwasher but sometimes it was quicker to wash by hand if there weren't too many.

When she'd finished, Zoe had stacked all the chairs on the tables and was busy vacuuming the floor. Annie sat in her cat bed, 'supervising'.

Zoe switched off the vacuum. "When are we going to arrange another playdate for Annie and AJ?"

"Brrt?" Annie asked, her ears pricked and green eyes shining.

AJ was a Maine Coon cat that Annie had found in the garden. Ed had instantly fallen in love with the tiny scrap of a kitten, and had adopted her on the spot, becoming a proud cat dad. But now she was sixteen months old and had grown into a much bigger cat. Sometimes, AJ came over to play with Annie, Zoe usually chauffeuring AJ from Ed's house to theirs.

"Whenever they'd like to," Lauren replied. "As long as it's okay with Ed."

"I'll ask him tomorrow."

"Brrt!" Annie seemed to agree.

Lauren took a last look around the empty café. Pale yellow walls, decorated with a string-art picture of a cupcake with lots of pink frosting – evidence of one of Zoe's former hobbies – gave the space a light and welcoming air.

Lauren locked the café and they walked through the private hallway to the cottage kitchen. After a dinner of spaghetti bolognaise, they spent the rest of the evening watching a relationship drama on TV, Lauren wondering how quickly Edna's murder would be solved.

CHAPTER 5

The next day, Zoe pounced on Ed as soon as they arrived in the café at eight o'clock. Pastry tins rattled in the kitchen, signaling his presence.

A minute later, Zoe zoomed out of the kitchen, a big smile on her face. "Ed said anytime is good with him for the play date."

"When would you like to have AJ come over, Annie?" Lauren asked the cat, who sat in her basket.

"Brrt," Annie replied, washing a paw.

"I think I'll have to guess what that means." Zoe giggled.

"I'm having dinner with Mitch tonight," Lauren told her.

"If he's picking you up, I could borrow your car," Zoe proposed.

"Of course." Lauren nodded.

"But I don't want you to miss out on watching them play together. They're so cute."

"I know." Usually, Annie and AJ ran through the cottage, exploring each room, then cuddled up together, either having a snooze, or sharing Annie's toys. They both seemed partial to Annie's small stuffed hedgehog, with the toy taking a nap with them, nestled between their two furry bodies.

"What about if I run over to Ed's straight after we close?"

"That would work," Lauren agreed.

"Annie?" Zoe cocked an eyebrow in the feline's direction.

"Brrt." *Yes.*

"Then it's all settled."

"As long as Ed knows."

"Oh, yeah." Zoe zipped back to the kitchen.

As soon as the clock hit nine-thirty, Lauren unbolted the oak and glass entrance door, ready for their first customer.

She glanced at the row of pottery mugs on the counter. She hoped Zoe wouldn't be disappointed if they didn't sell quickly.

The first part of the morning passed fairly slowly. What would she wear on her date with Mitch tonight? She didn't have an extensive wardrobe and tended to wear the same outfits on social occasions, just as she wore a work uniform of pale blue capris and apricot or peach t-shirts in the café. Zoe usually wore jeans or capris and brightly colored t-shirts, and they both wore aprons sometimes.

She'd already worn her plum wrap dress on Saturday night before – her mind shied away from what had happened after they returned to the B&B. What about—

"Hello."

Lauren blinked as Donna and Barbara greeted her. They stood at the *Please Wait to be Seated* sign.

"Hi," Lauren replied, her eyes widening.

"Brrt?" Annie ambled over to them, her eyes inquisitive.

"Isn't she adorable, Barbara?" Donna nudged her sister.

"She certainly is." Barbara bent down. "Hello."

"Annie will show you to a table," Lauren told them. "Just follow her."

"Ohh, so this is Annie." Donna nodded as she and her sister followed the feline through the café.

"Who are they?" Zoe whispered.

"Donna and Barbara." Lauren kept her voice low. "From—"

"The B&B!" Zoe's dark eyebrows climbed all the way up her forehead to meet her brunette pixie bangs.

"Yes," Lauren murmured.

"What are they here for? What do they want?"

"A latte or a cappuccino? I did mention the café to them."

"They're coming over."

Each table sported a menu, and on the menu was a request to please order at the counter. They relaxed the rule for the elderly, infirm, or harried.

Annie had strolled back to her bed, an alert expression on her face as she surveyed the quiet café. Apart from the sisters, there were only two other customers, and they were eating and drinking with apparent enjoyment.

"What do you recommend?" Donna asked as she approached the counter.

"Everything is delicious," Zoe told her. "Hi, I'm Zoe, Lauren's cousin."

The sisters introduced themselves, and ordered a large latte each, an apricot

Danish for Donna, and a triple chocolate ganache cupcake for Barbara.

"What brings you down here?" Zoe asked curiously as Lauren ground the beans for the espresso.

"We thought we'd take a little drive and check out your café," Donna replied with a flap of her hand. "Our weekend was cut short by—" she lowered her voice "—you know."

"The poor woman," her sister sympathized. "And her poor husband. He seemed such a nice man."

"Yes, he did," Lauren agreed. She wondered how Harry was coping at a time like this and hoped he had family to turn to.

"Donna took the day off," Barbara continued.

"I love taking time off work." Zoe plated the baked goods. "We're closed from Saturday lunchtime 'til Tuesday mornings."

"I'm fortunate that I don't have to work," Barbara told them.

"Is it usually so quiet on a Wednesday?" Donna broke in, looking around the room.

"No, usually it's pretty busy," Zoe told them a little defensively. "We had plenty of customers yesterday, and I've already sold some of my mugs. Look." She gestured to the mugs lined up along the counter, her motion worthy of a TV show presenter.

"They're certainly ... different." Barbara picked one up, frowning as she turned it around in her hands. She traced the small bulge at the side.

"I made them myself," Zoe informed them. "I painted Annie's portrait on one side. See?" She leaned over the counter and tapped Annie's likeness.

"That's very enterprising," Donna remarked.

"Thanks." Zoe beamed.

"We can bring your order over to you," Lauren told them, as she finished making a peacock design on the second latte.

"Thank you." Donna led the way to their table.

Annie remained in her cat bed. Had she sensed that the sisters didn't want her company?

"Have you heard any more from that detective?" Donna asked as she studied her latte. "This design is very clever."

"Thank you." She and Zoe had attended an advanced latte art class last year, and were now experienced making swans and peacocks, as well as the usual hearts, tulips, and rosettas that bloomed on the surface of the micro foam.

"No, she hasn't heard from Detective Castern," Zoe answered for her. "Have you?"

"Zoe!" Although, Lauren was curious about their answer.

"Not yet." Barbara shook her head, then stirred her latte.

"We were so excited when we won – well, Barbara won the prize," Donna told them. "And our suite was so beautiful. It looked just like the brochure. Did yours?"

"Yes." Lauren nodded, the image of their perfect room arising in her mind. "I loved the lavender shower gel in the bathroom. Did you try that?"

"We had rose scented gel," Barbara replied. "Poor Donna didn't get a chance to try it. I was actually taking a shower when the murder happened."

"No way," Zoe breathed.

"I'm afraid so." Barbara sighed. "When I shut off the water, I heard Donna screaming and came outside to see what was wrong. I never expected it to be poor Edna."

"It was just horrible." Donna shuddered and wrapped her hands around her mug. "Maybe we shouldn't talk about it anymore."

"But it's good to get these things off our chest." Barbara patted her sister's back. "We should let it all out, so it doesn't build up inside us."

"That's true," Zoe agreed. "Were you allowed to go home on Saturday night like Lauren and Mitch were?"

"Yes." Donna nodded. "I'm afraid I didn't like the detective who questioned us, but he told us to go straight home after taking our phone numbers and addresses. And in my case, my employer's details as well. If he has any more questions for me, I hope he's not going to show up at my work."

"I should hope not." Barbara frowned. "He should know it would be easy to find you – or me. We live together in Sacramento," she told Lauren and Zoe.

"It's only temporary," Donna said. "A bit of bad luck. I'm fortunate that Barbara has room for me."

"And for—"

"Oh look, your cat is coming over to us." Donna swiveled in her chair.

Annie padded toward them.

"Brrt?" she asked, sitting on the floor next to Lauren and Zoe, who stood at the table.

"I think she's asking if you're enjoying your order," Lauren explained.

"The coffee is wonderful," Donna enthused.

"And so is my triple chocolate cupcake," Barbara added.

Lauren and Zoe left the sisters to enjoy their treats, while Annie hopped up on a chair and joined the sisters.

"Don't you think it's strange they came all the way here from Sacramento?" Zoe asked as they reached the counter.

"Yes." Lauren nodded. Maybe the sisters were curious about her café as they had claimed, and had been at a loose end. She'd been disappointed too that her romantic weekend had been cut short – in such a horrible way – so it was entirely feasible the sisters felt the same way.

"Maybe they couldn't resist checking out Annie," Zoe continued. She glanced over at the sisters' table. Annie still sat on the chair, appearing to listen to their conversation, which consisted of a low murmur as well as a few admiring glances directed to the feline.

"That could be true." Lauren smiled.

Before they could mull over the sisters' appearance some more, the door opened and Ms. Tobin entered.

"Brrt!" Annie jumped off the chair and trotted to greet the newcomer.

Ms. Tobin had once been their prickliest customer, but she had mellowed in recent months, ever since Lauren and Zoe had warned her she was being scammed online. Tall, thin, and in her fifties, she used to wear outfits in depressing shades of brown. Now, her wardrobe consisted of lighter colors and more flattering shades. Today she wore an attractive amber dress and looked cool and comfortable.

"Hello, Annie, dear." Ms. Tobin smiled slightly as she greeted the cat. "Where should I sit?"

"Brrt." Annie waved her silver plumy tail and threaded her way through the tables until she reached one in the middle of the room.

"Thank you, Annie." Ms. Tobin sat down at the small table. Annie hopped up on the opposite chair. "Lauren, could I have a word with you please?" she called a trifle imperiously.

"Uh oh," Zoe muttered. "Don't tell me the old Tobin is here." Prickly Ms. Tobin had not been Zoe's favorite customer; in fact, Lauren had wondered if Zoe had been a little afraid of her. Now, they were both enjoying the more relaxed Ms. Tobin, and Lauren suspected Annie was, too.

"Hello." Lauren headed toward the table for two.

"Lauren," Ms. Tobin lowered her voice, "what is this I hear about a murder you were mixed up in? My friend found out about it at the senior center."

Martha, Lauren assumed, had spread the news.

"I was at a bed and breakfast last weekend in Zeke's Ridge," Lauren told her. "I'd won a prize in a contest."

"Oh, yes, I heard about that. I know you're seeing Detective Denman and you two went away together. I hope you're not a suspect."

"So do I," Lauren said ruefully.

"But if Detective Denman was with you, I would assume you would both be above suspicion."

"I hope so," Lauren replied, not sure if Ms. Tobin approved of her being at a B&B with Mitch, or not.

"And what about these mugs that have Annie's picture on them? I must see them." Ms. Tobin's expression changed from serious to curious.

"They're over there." Lauren gestured to the row of mugs on the counter. "Zoe made them. She's sold some already."

"I'll come over and take a look." Ms. Tobin followed Lauren to the array of cakes and pastries displayed temptingly in the sparkling clean glass case.

"Hi, Ms. Tobin," Zoe greeted her.

The older woman picked up a mug and studied it, turning it around in her hands.

"Oh yes, it does look like Annie." Ms. Tobin glanced from the mug to her table where Annie remained, and then back at the mug. "Quite rustic looking." She traced the slight bulge near the handle, then slid three fingers into the handle and lifted it toward her mouth. "I must have this one."

"Awesome." Zoe's eyes lit up. "Thank you."

"I do admire your crafting enthusiasm, Zoe," Ms. Tobin remarked. After putting in an order for a large latte and vanilla cupcake, she went back to her table – and Annie.

"Four sold!" Zoe high-fived Lauren. "I'm definitely going to make more mugs."

"I'm happy for you." And Lauren was.

"Now, let's see, I've added up all the costs, and then there's the price of my pottery classes, plus I need to pay the café a commission – twenty percent?" Zoe proposed.

"You don't have to pay me – the café," Lauren objected. Since Lauren owned the café, she paid each of them including herself, a decent wage, and Zoe and Ed shared the tip jar.

"Of course I should." Zoe shooed away her protest. "It's the cost of doing business. After my crochet cozy disaster a while ago, I decided to work out my costs properly this time. I'll still make a small profit on each mug that's sold for fifteen dollars."

"That's very professional of you." Lauren smiled. "I'll put the commission straight into the café's bank account."

"Now we're both being professional." Zoe giggled.

More customers arrived and the three of them were kept busy until after the lunch rush. Donna and her sister left before noon, saying goodbye and promising to visit again.

When Lauren and Zoe finally got a chance to take a break, they flopped on the stools behind the counter, Lauren wiggling her feet in her white sneakers.

"Phew!" Zoe fanned herself.

"Business was good this morning after all," Lauren commented.

"Yeah." Zoe nodded. "Hope you won't be too tired for your date tonight." She winked.

"Hope you won't be too tired to pick up AJ for her playdate with Annie," Lauren parried with a smile.

"No way." Zoe grinned.

When it was time to close up, Zoe zoomed around the room, stacking the chairs on the tables, while Annie watched with interest.

"I'll go and pick up AJ now," she called out after putting the vacuum away.

"Okay." Lauren emerged from the commercial kitchen.

"See you at the cottage. You too, Annie," she told the cat.

"Brrt!" Annie's mouth seemed to tilt up in a little smile.

"I'm having dinner with Mitch tonight," Lauren told her once Zoe had banged the back door shut. "But Zoe will be home with you."

"Brrp," Annie replied.

She knew Annie enjoyed her play time with AJ. A little while ago, Zoe had had the idea that AJ might like to train as Annie's assistant. However, the young

Maine Coon had different ideas, and her training period had been very short. But Annie and AJ still seemed to be the best of friends, which was the most important thing.

"Let's go and wait for AJ in the cottage," Lauren suggested.

"Brrt!" Annie led the way down the private hallway.

"We're here!" A short while later, Zoe appeared in the kitchen, carrying a cage.

"Meow!" A large, fawn tabby with dark brown stripes peered through the wire squares of the carrier. In the middle of her forehead was more dark brown fur in the shape of an M.

"Brrt!" Annie trotted over to her.

"Here you go, AJ." Zoe unfastened the top of the carrier, and the cat jumped out and greeted Annie.

"Brrt!" Annie raced from the room, AJ hot on her paws.

"So cute!" Zoe beamed as the sound of little feet pounding the carpet reached them.

"I know." Lauren nodded. "What are you and Annie going to do while I'm out with Mitch?"

"The usual," Zoe replied. "Have our own dinner, watch TV."

"When are you seeing Chris again?" Lauren asked.

"Next weekend." Zoe wrinkled her nose. "He's got a lot of shifts this week. I told him about my mugs, though, and he said he'd buy one. But I told him I'd give him one." A soft smile touched her lips.

"That's great." Her cousin had briefly investigated the world of online dating a while ago, and after some disastrous dates, had sworn off having a love life altogether. Until Chris came along. Funnily enough, he had been connected to one of her online dates, in a totally innocent way. Zoe had met him for the first time in person, as a friend of Mitch's.

"I'd better put one away for him, since they're starting to sell," Zoe said.

"Good idea."

Lauren and Zoe peeked into the living room. Annie and AJ were now chasing a tinkling ball around the room.

"That should keep them busy for a while," Zoe commented. She peeked at Lauren's white practical wrist watch.

"You'd better get ready for your date. What time is Mitch arriving – seven?"

"Yes." Lauren hurried to the bathroom and took a quick shower. She still hadn't decided what to wear.

When she entered her room, Zoe was already in there, rifling through her closet.

"Zoe?"

"I thought I'd help you get ready. Besides, I don't have anything else to do right now."

"What do you think?" Lauren gestured to the dresses hanging on the white plastic hangers.

"Not your plum wrap dress. You wear that a lot. It looks good on you, though."

"Gee, thanks."

"What about this?" Zoe pulled out a periwinkle outfit. "It's similar in style to your plum dress."

"Okay. Thanks." She wanted to quickly blow dry her hair, and grab her purse before Mitch arrived.

"Where are you two going?" Zoe asked.

"The bistro." It was one of their favorite places and was located on the outskirts of Gold Leaf Valley.

"I need Chris to live here, and then we can eat there whenever we feel like it." Zoe tapped her cheek. "And go to the Italian place again at Zeke's Ridge. And then we could double date with you and Mitch like we did when we visited the farmers' market in Sacramento a few months ago."

"Have you spoken to Chris about this?" Lauren asked as she zipped up her dress and grabbed the hairdryer. "Maybe he could look into transferring down here."

"No." Zoe shook her head. "It's probably a crazy idea." She sounded a little wistful, which was unlike her usual upbeat self.

"I thought you liked visiting him in Sacramento." They seemed to take turns visiting each other.

"Yes, I do," Zoe replied, "and going to restaurants there is fun. There's so much to choose from, compared to here, but I see your eyes light up when Mitch stops by the café."

"They do?" Lauren touched the gold L necklace he'd given her as she studied her hair in the mirror.

"Uh-huh."

"Chris visits you at the café sometimes," Lauren pointed out.

"That's true." Zoe sounded brighter.

It seemed that things might be getting serious between Zoe and Chris. They'd attempted to downplay their attraction to each other at the beginning, but she knew Zoe wasn't interested in seeing anyone else, and although she couldn't speak for Chris, she didn't think he was dating anyone else, either.

"Why don't you talk to him about it?" Lauren suggested, hoping she was doing the right thing. She didn't want to interfere in their relationship, especially if wanting to help them backfired.

"Maybe." Zoe sounded noncommittal.

Lauren finished getting ready. The doorbell rang just as she'd grabbed her purse.

"I'd better say goodbye to Annie and AJ. What time are you going to take AJ home?" Lauren asked.

"Probably straight after you've gone. Annie could come with us."

"She might like that," Lauren replied, heading to the front door and opening it.

"Hi." Mitch smiled. His tall, muscular frame filled out his charcoal slacks and gray dress shirt nicely. Lauren's heart fluttered.

"Hi." She returned his smile.

"Come in," Zoe called. "Lauren wants to say goodbye to Annie."

"No problem." He followed Lauren into the living room.

Annie and AJ were curled up together on the sofa, the small toy hedgehog nestled between them. Each of them had a paw resting on the hedgehog's brown furry stomach.

"Ohhh." Zoe's voice was hushed.

"I know." Lauren blinked fiercely. So cute.

"I've got to take a photo." Zoe zipped to her room and came back in the next second, waving her phone.

Click. The two cats didn't stir.

Zoe held out the phone to Lauren. She'd captured the sweet image perfectly.

Mitch peered over Lauren's shoulder at the screen.

"Yeah," he said. "I think that one's a keeper."

CHAPTER 6

At the bistro with its rustic but charming décor, Lauren ordered her favorite pork with four varieties of apples, while Mitch ordered steak with mushroom sauce.

"Has Detective Castern stopped by the café to ask you any more questions?" he asked as they waited for their entrees to arrive.

"No," she replied. "But Donna and her sister visited today." She told him what had transpired that morning. "Did you know that they live in Sacramento?"

"No." He shook his head. "That's where Edna and Harry used to live. But it's a big enough city, as we both know."

Their order arrived and they talked about more pleasant topics, until dessert.

Lauren decided to try the new cherry ice-cream, while Mitch opted for chocolate brownie.

"I've been put on another case," he told her as he dug his spoon into the large chocolatey square. He held it out to her, offering her a bite. Lauren shook her head. For some reason she didn't feel like chocolate right now. Perhaps because she'd had a triple chocolate cupcake during her break that afternoon.

"Want to try?" She held out a spoon of ice-cream to him, which he accepted. She watched his eyes narrow in concentration, then widen slightly in appreciation.

"It's good," he told her. "I hope they keep it on the menu."

She tested a small spoonful. "Me too." The cold smoothness of the ice-cream contrasted with the fruity flavor of the cherries.

After a few mouthfuls, she recalled what he'd just said.

"What sort of case is it?" she asked.

He looked like he was trying to hold back a wry chuckle.

"Garden gnomes."

"Is someone stealing them?"

"Yeah." He nodded. "From people's gardens."

"I've never noticed any around Gold Leaf Valley," she replied.

"Me neither," he agreed, "until they suddenly disappeared. I've had five reports of missing gnomes in the local area."

"That is so strange."

"Tell me about it. At least it's a bit of a change."

"So Detective Castern still doesn't want you on Edna's murder?"

"He wants to solve it on his own." His mouth tightened. "And since I was there, he says he needs to treat me as a suspect, the same as anyone else."

"But that's not right." Lauren looked at him in consternation.

"Yeah." He put down his spoon, a small portion of chocolate brownie remaining on the plate with half-melted vanilla ice-cream trickling over the top. "So be aware if he visits you at the café or at home. If he's thinking of me as a suspect, he's definitely thinking the same way about you."

When Mitch took her home, Lauren was still rattled by his pronouncement. He walked her up the porch steps and tenderly kissed her good night.

"I'm sorry about what happened last weekend at the B&B," he said.

"Me too." Lauren tried not to picture Edna's body lying in the hallway.

"Maybe we can plan another weekend away," he suggested.

"Not Zeke's Ridge," Lauren replied.

"No," he agreed. "But keep it in mind. It doesn't have to be right away."

She nodded, reaching up on tiptoe and kissing *him* goodnight.

When she entered the cottage, she realized she hadn't wondered if Annie or Zoe were spying on her and Mitch from one of the windows. It wouldn't have been the first time. But when she peeked in the living room, Zoe and Annie were both dozing on the sofa.

"Asleep already?" Lauren asked in a low voice.

"What? Oh, hi." Zoe blinked, opening her eyes and stretching. Annie lay curled up in a ball beside her. "I think Annie's worn out from her playdate. The movie was boring so I closed my eyes for a second." She looked chagrined. "I think it was a lot longer than that."

Lauren told her briefly about the garden gnome thefts, and to let her know if she saw Detective Castern around. Then she scooped up Annie, still fast asleep, and carried her to her bedroom. They usually slept together, Lauren inside the covers, and Annie on top of them.

"Brrt," Annie said sleepily as she curled in a tighter ball on top of the bedspread. *Good night.*

"Good night," Lauren echoed, sliding under the sheet and hoping for sweet dreams.

CHAPTER 7

The next morning, Annie woke her up by sitting on her stomach.

"Brrt," she greeted Lauren.

"Is it time to get up already?" Lauren blinked her eyes awake. She hadn't heard the alarm.

"Brrt." *Yes.*

She stumbled to the kitchen and fed Annie, then stepped into the shower, hoping the warm water would wake her up. Although she hadn't had sweet dreams, she hadn't experienced nightmares either, just a deep, dreamless sleep.

At breakfast she told Zoe more about her conversation with Mitch last night.

"Maybe someone's building a gnome garden," Zoe joked. "It's a shame Mitch isn't investigating Edna's death and Detective Castern isn't chasing down gnome thieves."

"Mm," Lauren agreed gloomily.

They finished getting ready, then went next door to the café.

"Maybe I should think up a new cupcake flavor," Lauren suggested.

The faint clang of pastry tins signaled Ed was already in the kitchen, hard at work.

"Good idea." Zoe's eyes lit up. "That might cheer us up."

Lauren decided to think up new summer flavors for the rest of the morning, and take her mind off Edna's murder.

But unfortunately, Detective Castern stood outside the café, right on the dot of nine-thirty.

"Oh, no." Lauren froze in the motion of unbolting the big oak door.

"Brrt?" Annie trotted up to her and peered through the plate glass. "Brrp." She sounded disapproving.

"Exactly," Lauren told her. "But we must be polite to him."

"Brrp," Annie grumbled, ambling back to her bed.

"What is it?" Zoe leaned across the counter.

Lauren tilted her head in the direction of the street outside.

"No way!" Zoe's eyes rounded.

"Yep." Lauren slowly finished unbolting the door.

"Good morning," Detective Castern greeted her as he strode into the café.

"Hi, Detective Castern," Zoe spoke up. "Would you like a latte? Cappuccino? Mocha?"

"No, thank you. I would like to speak to Lauren – Ms. Crenshaw."

"Yes?" Lauren said politely.

He scanned the empty room and took out his notebook, flipping it open.

"I have some follow up questions for you," he told her.

She nodded.

"What time did you get back to the bed and breakfast from your dinner at the Italian restaurant in Zeke's Ridge?" he asked.

Lauren was sure he'd asked her that on Saturday night.

"Around nine-thirty," she answered pleasantly.

"And then what did you do?"

She told him she and Mitch entered the foyer, and spoke to Harry for a moment.

"Was Harry already in the foyer when you stepped inside?" he asked.

"No. I don't think so," Lauren replied. "It all happened so quickly. I remember feeling startled that Harry was suddenly there." She hoped she hadn't said anything to make Harry a target in the detective's eyes. She'd liked Edna's husband and couldn't see him as a killer. She hoped he wasn't one.

"That will be all for now." Detective Castern flipped shut his notebook. "I may come back later."

Lauren nodded, glad there hadn't been any early customers to witness her questioning.

"Phew," Zoe said after he'd left and the door had shut behind him.

"Exactly."

"Brrt!" Annie agreed from her cat bed.

"Hopefully he won't come back again," Zoe said. "Now all we need are a ton of customers to take your mind off his questions."

As if on cue, the door opened, and Hans stepped inside.

"Brrt!" Annie ran to greet him.

"Hello, *Liebchen*." The dapper man in his sixties bent stiffly to greet her.

"Hi, Hans." Lauren smiled at one of their favorite customers.

"Hello, Lauren, hello, Zoe," he replied, smiling at them. "Where shall I sit, Annie, hmm?"

"Brrt." *This way.* Annie strolled toward a four-seater near the counter, as if she knew that Hans couldn't hurry after her.

"Ach, thank you, *Liebchen*." Hans sat down on the pine chair. Annie hopped up on the one next to him.

"What can we get you?" Lauren headed toward his table.

"A cappuccino I think today."

"Ed's made honeyed walnut Danishes, and apricot pastries," Zoe announced, joining them as well.

"And I've got vanilla, cinnamon swirl, and orange poppyseed cupcakes," Lauren added.

"How am I going to decide?" Hans' faded blue eyes twinkled. "And I must have one of these mugs with Annie's picture on them. I've heard a lot about them."

"Really?" Zoe looked delighted. "I'll bring one over to you." She raced to the counter, grabbed a pottery mug and raced back.

"*Ja*, it is very nice." Hans studied the cup. "Look, Annie, your face is on this side." He held out the mug to her.

"Brrt." Annie seemed pleased as she looked at her portrait on the mug.

Hans ordered a honeyed walnut pastry along with his cappuccino.

"Now I've sold five," Zoe crowed as she and Lauren walked back to the counter. "Maybe pottery really *is* the hobby for me."

"You could be right," Lauren agreed. Sometimes Zoe's crafting efforts ended in disappointment – she was just glad that so far that hadn't happened with pottery.

They took over Hans' order. He was their only customer, and he invited them to sit down.

"I have also heard about this murder at Zeke's Ridge," he said as he sipped his coffee. "Are you all right, Lauren? Mitch was with you, *ja*?"

"*Ja* – I mean yes." Lauren's cheeks grew hot. Did everyone in the small town know she'd gone away for a weekend with Mitch? Probably.

"Then there should not be a problem," Hans said. "Mitch will solve the case and catch the killer."

"It's not so simple as that," Zoe told him, wearing a glum expression. They told him about Detective Castern.

"That is not *gut*." Hans shook his head. "I just hope he can solve this crime."

"So do I," Lauren agreed, also hoping that the detective didn't really consider her or Mitch suspects.

More customers arrived, and they left Annie sitting with Hans.

"Oh, we forgot to tell him about garden gnomes disappearing." Zoe tapped her cheek. "I wonder if Hans has one in his yard?"

"We'll tell him when he leaves," Lauren proposed, already steaming milk for a large latte.

"Maybe we should buy one," Zoe proposed, her brown eyes sparkling. "We could put it in our garden and then catch the thief!"

"What if it's stolen while we're serving customers?" Lauren pointed out the hole in her cousin's plan.

"We could set up a camera to record anyone coming into the garden," Zoe countered.

"How much is that going to cost?"

"Ooh, I know! Maybe the police department could pay for it – and the gnome. It could be a sting operation."

"Do you think we're watching too many crime shows?" Lauren asked.

"With all the crime happening everywhere, I don't think we're watching enough!"

CHAPTER 8

"Ooh, I'm going to tell Mitch my idea!" Zoe's eyes lit up as Mitch strode into the café that afternoon.

Pleasure flitted across her face as she noticed the guy following Mitch into the shop.

"Chris!"

"Hi." Chris smiled at her. "My shift finished early so I thought I'd stop by and see you."

"Good." Zoe's eyes softened as she looked at him.

Mitch cleared his throat. "We bumped into each other outside."

"Why don't we all sit down for a minute?" Lauren proposed. There were only two customers in the café, and they were busy drinking their lattes and enjoying their cupcakes.

"Brrt!" Annie agreed as she trotted up to them. "Brrt!" *This way!*

They followed Annie to a six-seater at the rear.

"We can get you something in a minute," Zoe told them. "Mitch, I've got a great idea!" She scraped back the pine chair and sat down.

"What is it?" Chris looked interested.

Zoe filled the two guys in on her plan to catch the gnome thief. Annie sat on one of the chairs next to Lauren, looking interested in the conversation.

"It sounds pretty good to me." Chris glanced at Mitch.

"I think so, too." Mitch replied. "I'll see what I can do to make it happen. But Zoe, don't get discouraged if the thief doesn't bite. There doesn't seem to be any rhyme or reason to the gardens he's targeting."

"I won't," Zoe promised, but Lauren noticed the spark of excitement in her eyes. She hoped the thief would target them, just so Zoe wouldn't be disappointed if her plan didn't work.

"I might be able to set up the cameras tomorrow, if it's approved," Mitch added.

"Don't forget the gnome." Zoe giggled.

"Where do you buy gnomes from, anyway?" Lauren asked.

"A garden center, I guess," Zoe answered. "Maybe there's a gnome shortage going on and that's why they're getting stolen!"

"I'll see if I can buy one," Mitch said. "I'll keep you posted."

They made Mitch and Chris a large latte each. Mitch took his to go, but Lauren shooed Zoe back to Chris's table, where Annie remained.

"Enjoy some time with him," she told her cousin.

"Thanks, boss." Zoe grinned. She made herself a mocha and joined Chris and Annie.

Lauren glanced over at Zoe and Chris. They were deep in conversation, Zoe looking happy and animated. So was Chris. It would be great if he could get a transfer to Gold Leaf Valley – if that was what he wanted.

The rest of the afternoon sped by until with a start she realized it was five o'clock. Chris had departed about an hour ago and Zoe had filled her in on their plans to have dinner together Saturday night.

"I told him I couldn't do Friday night, because it's craft club."

"I feel the same with Mitch," Lauren told her. On Friday evenings, the three of them visited Mrs. Finch's house for craft club, a Zoe invention. Since Zoe's list of hobbies seemed to change monthly, at times it had been referred to as knitting club, crochet club, string-art club, beading club and now, pottery club. They'd recently agreed it might be easier just to call it craft club.

The two of them had started out with knitting, which Lauren had stuck to – although lately she'd had trouble making up her mind what to knit next. So far, she'd knitted a hat and scarf for herself – and Mitch. Now it was summer, she didn't really feel like knitting at all, but she didn't know whether she was game to try her hand at anything else.

That evening, Zoe chatted about her upcoming plans with Chris. It was Zoe's turn to choose what they did and she wanted them to try a different cuisine – so far it was a toss-up between Nepalese and Moroccan.

"Maybe Annie could help me choose," Zoe mused as she sat at the kitchen table with Lauren after dinner.

"Where is she?" Lauren crinkled her brow. The feline had eaten her meal of beef in gravy earlier, and then had disappeared.

"Let's find out." Zoe jumped up from the table.

A second later, Lauren's eyes widened as she stood in the doorway of the living room.

Annie was on the carpet, and so was Lauren's phone. She'd put the device on the coffee table earlier.

"Brrt," Annie said, and pushed her tinkling ball toward the phone.

"Meow!" came a faint voice from the phone.

"Did Annie call AJ?" Lauren turned to look at Zoe.

"Or maybe AJ called Annie." Zoe giggled softly.

Lauren crept closer to Annie, who seemed unaware of their presence. She could see AJ on the phone screen.

"They're using the video app," Lauren told her cousin.

"No way!"

Lauren and Annie had checked in on Zoe using that phone app when Lauren had had a cold, and Zoe had been in charge of the café. And Lauren knew that Annie had called AJ on the phone previously to 'talk' to her, but this was the first time that she had seen Annie use the video app to call her friend.

"Meow," came AJ's voice from the other end. A jingle accompanied the sound and Lauren could see a red ball rolling past the screen.

"Are they each pushing their balls and showing each other what they're doing?" Zoe marveled.

"It looks like it." Lauren smiled.

"Brrt," Annie said to her friend on the screen, pushing her pink ball with her paw. *Tinkle.*

"AJ? What are you doing?" Ed's voice.

"Meow!"

"Hi Ed," Zoe called out.

"Zoe? Annie?" Ed's face loomed in the screen, auburn tufts of hair sticking up this way and that.

"Hi," Lauren said.

"Brrt!" Annie turned around to glance at Lauren and Zoe, then switched her attention back to the phone screen.

"I think Annie and AJ were enjoying a video chat." Zoe giggled. "Or a video play date."

"Really?" At first Ed sounded disbelieving, then he chuckled. "Why not? Annie is one smart cat. AJ, too."

"Brrp." *Thank you.*

While they'd been talking to Ed, Annie had fetched her small toy hedgehog. She held it in her mouth and tilted her head at the phone screen.

"Mew." AJ appeared a second later, holding a little stuffed bunny in her mouth, gray and white.

"I bought her that rabbit the other day," Ed told them. "She loves it."

"Just like Annie loves her hedgehog," Lauren remarked.

After a few more minutes of conversation, they left Annie and AJ to enjoy their 'play time'.

"No one would believe us if they hadn't seen it with their own eyes," Lauren said.

"I don't know," Zoe replied. "Surely we can't be the only ones who think that Annie can do anything?"

CHAPTER 9

The next day, Mitch entered the café with good news.

"Your sting operation has been approved, Zoe." He stifled a smile at her excited expression.

"Yes!" Zoe high-fived Lauren.

"The gnome is in my trunk. I just need to put it in your garden and set up the cameras."

"Ooh, what color is he – or she?" Zoe asked.

"He's red and yellow."

"But how will anyone know we've got a gnome in the rear garden?" Zoe frowned suddenly. "You can't see the back lawn from the front of the street. You'd have to go up the side of the café and turn the corner to take a look. Or should we put it in the small front garden?"

"That will be too exposed to the street," Mitch told them. "So far, the thief has stolen gnomes in obscured parts of gardens. I'm sure he cases the gardens first – and that's what we're counting on in this case."

Mitch left to set everything up, returning a short while later.

"Here's the camera feed." He showed them how to access it on their phones.

"The lawn looks a bit shaggy," Lauren murmured. She hadn't realized until now.

"Brrt?" Annie had wandered over to the counter. There weren't many customers at the moment.

"We're going to catch the gnome thief," Zoe told her. "Look!" She held out the phone to Annie.

"It's like when you had a video play date with AJ last night," Lauren added.

"Brrt." Annie stared at the screen, her green eyes wide.

"Nothing's happening right now," Lauren told her.

"But I hope it does!" Zoe added.

***

"We forgot to ask Mitch if he had any news about Edna's death," Lauren told her cousin a short while later. Mitch had left and the three of them had stared at the camera feed for a few minutes, until more customers trickled in.

"I'm sure he would have updated us if he knew anything," Zoe assured her. "I bet Detective Castern isn't sharing any information with him."

"You're probably right." Lauren shivered. She hoped the detective didn't return to question her again.

"You know, *we* should solve Edna's murder," Zoe told her as she plated a triple chocolate cupcake.

"You don't think Detective Castern is up to the task?"

"He hasn't caught the killer yet," Zoe pointed out.

"That we know of."

"The murder happened a week ago." Zoe tsked. "Why isn't it all over the front page of the newspaper that the killer was caught? I'm sure I read somewhere that it's a lot harder to catch the killer after the first forty-eight hours of an investigation."

"You sounded like Ms. Tobin just then." Lauren was amused despite herself.

Zoe shuddered. "No way! Although, I am enjoying the new mellower Ms. Tobin."

"So am I," Lauren agreed. She had been one of their few customers who hadn't deserted them when a cupcake rival had set up their truck right outside the café recently.

They chatted about their plans for the weekend. Zoe still hadn't made up her mind between Nepalese and Moroccan for her dinner with Chris tomorrow night. Lauren thought he would be surprised whatever restaurant Zoe chose.

Lauren and Mitch were still deciding what to do tomorrow night. She knew he would take her to dinner in Sacramento if that was what she wanted to do – in fact, why didn't they double date with Zoe and Chris? But as she looked at her cousin's glowing face as she pondered restaurant choices, Lauren thought Zoe might enjoy some alone time with Chris. She'd propose doubling another time.

Every few minutes, they glanced at the camera feed on the phone, but everything looked exactly the same.

"No thieves," Zoe said sadly as they closed at five.

"No," Lauren agreed, wondering if that was good or bad news.

Martha suddenly barreled into the café.

"Brrt!" Annie ran to greet her

Zoe looked at Lauren, her eyes sparkling. "Ooh, we should tell Martha we have a gnome in the garden. She might tell her friends down at the senior center."

"And they might tell their friends, mentioning it in passing ..." Lauren smiled slowly.

"And BAM! When the gnome thief hears about it, he'll try to steal our gnome!"

***

That night, they filled in Mrs. Finch on the gnome sting operation, including innocently telling Martha about their new garden decoration.

"She seemed to find the news very interesting." Lauren recalled how Martha had blinked in surprise when they told her about their gnome.

"My goodness," she exclaimed. "I hope you girls will be careful."

"Brrt!" Annie agreed. *Yes.*

Lauren explained her craft dilemma to Mrs. Finch.

"You could try crochet," Zoe suggested. "You could borrow my hook. And you might have some left-over wool from your scarves and hats. I think I used up all my yarn, but I'll check."

"Thanks," Lauren replied. "But I'm not sure if crochet is for me."

"What about string-art or making bead jewelry?" Zoe listed the other crafts she'd tried.

"What about embroidery?" Mrs. Finch suggested.

"Not that." Zoe shuddered. She was not known for her sewing skills.

"Brrt," Annie seemed to agree with Zoe.

"There's always pottery," Zoe suggested. "But you'd have to start off with making an ashtray, like I did. Or two ashtrays. I know! You could come to my pottery classes!" Her brown eyes lit up with enthusiasm.

"Thanks, but I'm not sure if clay would be my thing, either," Lauren replied with a smile. She knew her cousin enjoyed her classes in Sacramento and besides learning pottery skills, Zoe was able to visit Chris as well. Lauren didn't want to muscle in on that.

"I think for now I'll stick with knitting," Lauren added. "I'll just have to think up a new project."

CHAPTER 10

On Saturday afternoon, Mitch surprised her by turning up at the house.

"You're right, the lawn does look a little shaggy." He smiled.

They stood in the back garden surveying the rough grass.

Lauren thought he looked just as good dressed in an old pair of faded denim jeans and a gray t-shirt, as he did when he dressed up to take her out to dinner.

"I wasn't hinting when I said that."

"I know you weren't," he assured her.

"Any news about the gnome thief?" Lauren asked, looking up at him.

"No." He shook his head. "And the little guy is still here." He gestured to a spot near the brown wooden shed. The gnome dressed in a yellow jacket and red trousers stood looking coyly at them.

"Do you think anyone will try and steal him?"

"I hope so." He smiled at her and headed toward the shed. "I'll get started."

"How lucky am I, Annie?" The Norwegian Forest Cat suddenly appeared. Zoe and Annie knew she disliked mowing the lawn, a chore that Mitch had willingly undertaken a while ago.

"Brrt," Annie agreed, her long white whiskers seeming to vibrate in agreement.

Lauren sat down in the living room with a cozy mystery she'd decided to try, but found it hard to concentrate. The steady drone of the mower should have been comforting, but instead she felt guilty that she was relaxing – or attempting to – while Mitch was working in the garden – *her* garden. Perhaps she should join him?

At the very least she could have a nice cold drink ready for him. The afternoon was warm and sunny.

"Is that Mitch mowing out there?" Zoe appeared in the living room.

"Yes." Lauren rose from the sofa. "I'm going to make him some lemonade. Want some?"

"You bet." Zoe grinned. "I was sorting through my closet but didn't find any left-over yarn for you."

"That's okay." Lauren smiled. "I still haven't decided what to knit next, anyway."

"What about a blanket for Annie?" she suggested. "It might be finished when the colder weather hits."

"But you knitted two blankets for Annie," Lauren reminded her.

"Ooh, a tea cozy!" Zoe's eyes sparkled. "When someone orders a pot of tea at the café – okay, not many of our customers do – you could put it on the teapot and it might be a talking point – especially among the seniors."

"That *is* an idea," Lauren said slowly. And it wouldn't be a huge project. It mightn't take her very long to make. "Okay, why not?"

"Awesome!" Zoe grinned.

"Brrt?" Annie asked.

"I'm going to make a tea cozy," Lauren told her.

"Brrp." Annie sounded a little unsure about *that*.

They all entered the kitchen. Lauren got out lemons, sugar, and filled a pitcher with water.

"I know I should cook the lemon juice and sugar," she told Zoe, "but I want it to be ready by the time Mitch needs a break from out there." She nodded toward the back door.

"I'm sure he won't mind," Zoe told her. "In fact, I think he'd eat and drink anything you made for him – even if it didn't taste good!"

"Zoe!" Lauren stifled a smile, touching the gold L of her necklace.

"So when are you two going on another romantic weekend?" Zoe teased. "Since your first one ended in murder." She sobered.

"We haven't talked about it much," Lauren replied. Mitch had been occupied with his gnome case, and she and Zoe had been busy running the café. Besides, was it only one week ago that they'd been at the B&B at Zeke's Ridge? It seemed a lot longer than that.

"We should check it out," Zoe told her.

"Check out what?" Lauren crinkled her brow as she juiced the lemons.

"Brrt?" Annie queried.

"The B&B. Edna's husband."

"You think?" Lauren measured out the sugar.

"Yes." Zoe sounded a little exasperated. "Like I said before, I don't think Detective Castern is going to solve this case, so it's up to us – again."

"I don't think it would look good for Mitch if Detective Castern finds out Mitch's girlfriend was poking about in his murder case." Lauren stirred the juice and sugar concoction.

"You haven't seemed to worry about that before." Zoe frowned.

Lauren put down the wooden spoon and faced her cousin.

"Do you really think we need to go sleuthing?"

"Yes!"

"Brrt!"

Lauren looked at Zoe's animated face and Annie's hopeful one, and gave in – like she usually did.

"Okay, fine. We'll visit Harry and see how he's doing. But that's all."

"Of course." Zoe was all smiles. "Isn't that right, Annie?"

"Brrt." Annie looked as innocent as could be. "Brrt!"

***

A while later, Mitch came into the kitchen, all hot and sweaty. There was a smudge of dirt on his cheek and his short dark hair was matted at the temples. The aroma of freshly cut grass and sunshine surrounded him. Lauren thought he looked and smelled delectable.

"Here." She offered him a frosty glass of lemonade.

"Thanks." He downed it in one gulp.

She refilled the glass and held it out to him.

"I'll go home and have a shower, then pick you up at seven."

"Where are we going?" she asked.

"You choose."

"I don't want to go to Zeke's Ridge." She instantly felt guilty about her plan to visit Harry. Should she tell Mitch? She wanted to, but maybe it would be best if she didn't. That way, he could honestly tell Detective Castern that he knew nothing about it – if the detective found out about their little jaunt.

"I understand." He nodded.

She sighed. She loved living in this small town but there weren't a lot of restaurant choices. She didn't feel like burgers, and the former steak house wasn't an option right now. And she and Mitch had been to the bistro a lot recently.

"I don't know," she admitted.

"We can go to Sacramento," he told her.

"Maybe," she replied. Perhaps she should have suggested to Zoe they double date tonight after all.

Lauren didn't know what was wrong with her. She loved spending time with Mitch, even if it was just enjoying a latte together. Was it the fact that she hadn't made up her mind about their sleeping arrangements last weekend? Or the fact that it had been made up for her – by the killer?

"Let's do something different," she proposed.

"Like what?" A smile edged his mouth.

"Like—" she grabbed an old phone directory from the kitchen counter, closed her eyes and flicked it open. She stabbed her finger on a page and opened her eyes. "Like this … comedy club in Sacramento."

"I'm game if you are." He put down his glass. "Okay, I'll go home and grab a shower. See you at seven."

She nodded.

The doorbell rang.

"Expecting someone?" He raised an eyebrow.

"No."

"Brrt!" Annie had been silent during their conversation, as if taking it all in. Now, she scampered down the hall toward the front door.

Lauren followed her, wondering who it was. Zoe was getting ready for her date. Maybe Chris had driven over, wanting to surprise her? Or was it Father Mike, collecting for the local Episcopal Church?

She opened the door, conscious of Mitch standing behind her. Her mouth parted and her eyes widened.

"Mom!"

CHAPTER 11

A well-dressed woman of medium height stood in the doorway. Her brown hair was a slightly darker shade than Lauren's, threaded with gray.

"I'm guessing you're Mitch," Lauren's mother said, her hazel eyes seeming to take in everything about him.

"Yes, ma'am," Mitch replied. "I'm sorry you're seeing me like this, but I've just finished mowing the lawn."

A slight smile tipped her mother's mouth.

"Are you going to let me in, Lauren?" she asked.

"Sorry." Lauren stepped aside.

Her mother sailed into the house. "Hello, Annie." She bent down to gently stroke the silver-gray tabby. "Are you looking after Lauren?"

"Brrt," Annie replied, her head seeming to nod yes.

"Hi, Aunt Celia." Zoe suddenly appeared. "We weren't expecting you, but it's nice to see you."

"I know you girls are busy," Lauren's mother replied. "So I thought I'd surprise you. I hope I haven't come at the wrong time."

"Not at all, Mom." Lauren hugged her mother, feeling guilty that she hadn't visited her in a while. Her weekends had been taken up with dating Mitch and the occasional sleuthing mission.

"I see you're taking good care of your Gramms' house," Mrs. Crenshaw said with approval.

"We sure are." Zoe grinned. "And the café. Would you like a latte? I can make you one and put a peacock pattern on top of the micro foam."

"I've heard all about your swans and peacocks." Mrs. Crenshaw looked fondly at Lauren. "Why don't we sit down in the kitchen? You've told me about Mitch for a while now, Lauren, but this is the first time I've met him."

Lauren's cheeks flamed.

"Mitch is all hot and sweaty," she protested. "It's not really fair for you to meet him like this."

"Nonsense," her mother said, taking Mitch's measure as she eyed his tall, muscular frame covered in his grass-stained jeans and t-shirt. "I know you don't care much for yard work, so I think it's sweet of him to help you out like this."

"She made him lemonade," Zoe put in. "Brrt!"

"I'd love a glass if there's any left." Her mother swept into the kitchen.

Lauren sent Zoe a *help me* look.

Zoe just grinned.

"Where's Dad?" Lauren asked, as she hurried after her mother.

"Mowing *our* lawn, actually," she replied as she sat down at the large kitchen table. "Now, Mitch—" she patted the chair next to her "—tell me a little about yourself. Lauren says you're a police detective."

"That's right, Mrs. Crenshaw." Mitch sat down and smiled at the older woman.

Lauren shifted in her chair as her mother grilled Mitch – discreetly, of course. Had her mother found out or sensed somehow that she and Mitch had gone away on a romantic weekend together? But the topic didn't come up.

She glanced over at Zoe, who seemed amused at the interrogation – but she wondered if her cousin would still look like that if it was *her* mom interviewing Chris?

"I won't keep you three any longer." Mrs. Crenshaw finally rose from the table. "Now I know why you haven't come to Sacramento to visit your father and me so often lately, Lauren."

She flushed as she walked her mother to the door.

"Enjoy your evening with Mitch tonight, dear." Her mother smiled at her. "I think he's a keeper," she added in a low voice. "Especially if he's doing yard work for you without grumbling."

Lauren wondered if she'd inherited her lack of enthusiasm for mowing the lawn from her mother.

"Thanks, Mom." She hugged her.

Her mother held her tightly for a few seconds, then stepped back. "Maybe next time I visit I'll be able to meet Chris – I've heard about him from Zoe's mom."

Lauren nodded, wondering what Zoe would make of *that*.

***

They all had dates that Saturday night – Lauren and Mitch, Zoe and Chris – and Annie and AJ in a manner of speaking.

"What are you doing?" Lauren asked the cat as she waited for Mitch to arrive.

Annie put a paw out on the coffee table, reaching for Lauren's phone.

"Brrt." She hooked the cell onto the carpet and pressed a button.

"Are you going to video call AJ?" Lauren smiled.

"Brrt!" *Yes!*

A second later, a "meow" sounded from the other end and AJ's brown furry face came into view.

"Brrt," Annie chirped into the phone, lifting a paw as if waving hello to her friend.

"Mew!" AJ copied her friend, her paw in the air.

"Have fun," Lauren told her, wishing Zoe was here to witness the online play date. She'd already left for her date with Chris, borrowing Lauren's car. She still hadn't made up her mind where to take him, telling Lauren she'd decide on the drive there.

The doorbell rang and Lauren hurried to answer it. She hoped her mother's interrogation of Mitch that afternoon hadn't freaked him out. But when she opened the door, he smiled at her, stopping her heart completely.

"I'm glad I met your mom," he greeted her.

"I had no idea she was coming over."

"I know." He slipped his arms around her waist and drew her to him. "But I think it was past time I met her."

She melted in his arms, returning his kiss.

"All ready to go?" he murmured.

"I'll just say goodbye to Annie." She hurried into the living room, not wanting to disturb her if she was busy "chatting" with AJ.

Tinkle.

Annie pushed her pink ball, glancing at the phone screen as she did so.

A jingle echoed from the other end of the phone.

"Bye, Annie," Lauren called softly. The tabby barely looked up from her game of video play date.

"Brrp," she replied absently, pushing the ball forward again and looking at the screen.

***

Lauren enjoyed her date with Mitch – two of the comedians she didn't find funny, but the last one had her giggling nonstop. Mitch chuckled along with her.

"I'm glad we did something different," Lauren told him as they left the club.

"Me too." He smiled down at her as he held the car door open for her.

As Mitch drove them back to Gold Leaf Valley, she wondered if Zoe's date had been enjoyable as hers.

***

"What time is it?" Zoe dragged herself into the kitchen the next morning. Her pixie cut was disheveled, and her robe hung open, revealing red sleep shorts and matching t-shirt.

"Nine o'clock." Lauren crunched granola.

"Brrt?" Annie asked. She sat next to Lauren at the table.

"I had a great night, Annie." Zoe smiled. "I got to bed late, that's all."

"What time did you get in?" Lauren asked curiously. She'd gotten home first.

"One?" Zoe squinted, as if by doing that she could recall exactly what time it had been.

"Tell us all about it," Lauren invited. She'd filled Zoe in on her dates with Mitch in the past – as much detail as she'd been comfortable with, anyway.

"We had Ethiopian!"

"What happened to Nepalese or Moroccan?"

"I'd just about decided on Nepalese," Zoe explained, sinking down at the table, "when I drove past this little Ethiopian restaurant on the way to Chris's apartment. So I thought, why not? I bet he hasn't been there before!"

"Had he?"

"Nope." Zoe grinned. "We had spicy chickpeas and this amazing chicken and spices dish, and lots of rice. Then for dessert, we both felt like ice cream, so he took me to this incredible place – *we have got to go there* – and we had two scoops each! I had red velvet, and maple rhubarb, and he had cinnamon, and chocolate mint."

"Wow," Lauren murmured. She'd never heard of maple rhubarb ice-cream before. "Let's go next weekend."

"Deal." Zoe grinned. "We could double date! I checked the opening times and they're open on Sundays."

"I'll tell Mitch."

"And I'll tell Chris. And we could go to the farmers' market first, and then have ice cream for lunch."

"Brrt!"

***

Over an hour later, they set off to visit Harry at his bed and breakfast in Zeke's Ridge.

"I hope he doesn't mind us calling in," Lauren said as she drove through Gold Leaf Valley.

"I'm sure he won't," Zoe told her. "What do you think, Annie?"

"Brrt." Annie seemed to agree with Zoe. She sat in her carrier, strapped in the back, looking out the window at the passing rural scenery.

"Check out the gardens!" Zoe's eyes rounded as Lauren turned into the driveway, the tires crunching on the gravel. Pine trees, large green bushes, and the occasional clump of cheery yellow buttercups greeted them.

"I know," Lauren agreed, as she parked in front of the house. There were no other cars around.

"The house looks amazing." Zoe tilted her head as she stared at the old Victorian painted in cream with pale blue trim.

"What if he isn't home?" Lauren fretted.

"I don't think we have to worry about that." Zoe gestured to the older man coming down the porch steps. "Is that him?"

"Yes. What are we going to ask him?"

"Leave that to me." Zoe got out of the car.

"I hope Zoe knows what she's doing," Lauren murmured to Annie. She unstrapped Annie's carrier, freed her, and fastened her harness on her.

"Brrp?" Annie looked around the grounds with wide green eyes. Green bushes and big pine trees beckoned them to explore.

"Hi, Harry," Lauren called.

"Hello." Harry looked at them quizzically. "Oh, Lauren from last weekend. The B&B is closed right now." His voice broke at the end. "Excuse me."

"I'm Zoe, Lauren's cousin." Zoe held out her hand. "Lauren told me all about your place and I thought it sounded amazing. I'm sorry about your wife."

"Thank you." Harry nodded. His eyes sharpened as he noticed Annie standing next to Lauren. "Who's this?"

"This is my cat, Annie." Lauren gestured to the large silver-gray tabby. "I hope it's okay that she came with us."

"She wanted to see your place, too," Zoe told him engagingly.

"Of course." He smiled a little. "She certainly is a beautiful cat."

"Brrt." *Thank you.*

"Come in." He motioned toward the house. "Would you like a cup of tea – or coffee? I've got soda and juice as well. Edna always has – had – a well-stocked kitchen."

"That's very kind of you," Lauren replied, feeling guilty that they were here on a sleuthing mission. "A glass of water would be nice."

"I'd love some juice," Zoe replied. She entered the foyer after Harry. "Wow. This place is gorgeous." She gazed up at the chandelier, then looked over at the wooden mantel decorated with two silver candlesticks. "Lauren has a Victorian as well, but it's not nearly as big as this."

"It's just a cottage," Lauren replied.

"You're from Gold Leaf Valley," Harry said as he urged them to sit on the sofa in the foyer.

"That's right." Lauren nodded.

"Lauren said you're from Sacramento," Zoe remarked, sinking down on the plush antique sofa.

Annie sat primly on the floor next to Lauren's feet, surveying the room.

"Yes." Harry sighed. "It was Edna's dream to run a B&B and look what happened." He pressed his lips together, as if trying to control his emotions.

"I'm sorry," Lauren apologized. "Maybe this wasn't a good idea. We could go—"

"No." Harry shook his head. "It was good of you girls to drop by."

"What about your family?" Zoe asked.

Lauren frowned at her cousin's bluntness.

"We couldn't have children. That was why Edna enjoyed her job as a substitute teacher so much – she got to have children in her life that way. I have a brother in Arizona, but Edna was an only child."

"I'm sorry," Lauren said. She was beginning to think Zoe's idea of visiting Harry wasn't a good one. They shouldn't have intruded on his grief.

"I'll be back in a minute with your beverages." He left the room, exiting through the discreet inner door the same way he'd done that night when Lauren and Mitch had returned from the Italian restaurant – the night Edna was murdered.

"Are you sure about this?" she whispered to Zoe. Her cousin had jumped up from the sofa and was exploring the room. She picked up a brown book from the counter and leafed through it.

"Here's your entry in the guest register." She held out the book to Lauren.

"Put it back." Harry would return any moment.

"Who else signed this? Mitch, and—" Zoe squinted "—this handwriting is terrible! Donald – no, Donna. Oh, Donna and her sister who visited the café. The other winners."

"Yes," Lauren hissed. "Put it back, Zoe."

"Okay," Zoe grumbled, returning the book to the counter. "We *are* supposed to be sleuthing, you know."

"Maybe we shouldn't."

The side door opened and Harry came in, wheeling a little silver trolley.

"Edna's idea." He served them their drinks, then looked down at Annie. "I'm sorry, I didn't ask if your cat would like some water. We've got plenty of bowls – for breakfast, you know."

"I can share my water with Annie, if that's okay," Lauren told him. She took a sip, then put the glass down on the pale gold carpet, holding it so it wouldn't tip over. "Want some?" she softly asked the tabby.

"Brrp." *Thank you.* Annie delicately lapped at the water, her pink tongue darting in and out of the tumbler.

"Look at that," Harry marveled.

"Do you have pets?" Zoe asked.

"No." He shook his head. "I would have loved to have a dog, but Edna and I were at work all day and it didn't seem fair. I did think now that we were running this place together that we could get one, but then Edna—" his voice broke.

"I understand," Lauren told him, feeling extra guilty they were bothering the poor man. She didn't know about Zoe, but she was sure Harry was innocent.

"Have you heard from Detective Castern?" Zoe probed.

"A couple of days ago. He wanted to go over my statement again. I didn't have anything else to add. He particularly wanted to know where I was at the time of – the time of—" Harry buried his face in his hands.

Lauren glanced at Zoe. *We should leave.*

Not yet, Zoe's return glance said.

After a moment, Harry recovered. "I told him the same thing I told him on the night it happened." He took his hands away from his face. "I was in our living room. I didn't hear a thing – until you and Mitch arrived back here from dinner." He looked at Lauren.

"When was the last time you saw Edna before – you know?" Zoe asked.

"Zoe!" Lauren hissed.

"Brrt!" Annie sounded shocked as well. Lauren suspected she'd taken a liking to Harry.

"We were watching TV. Our quarters are through there." Harry pointed to the side door in the foyer. "Kitchen, living room, bedroom, and bathroom. There was a commercial, and Edna said she wanted to go upstairs and check on something."

"Like what?" Zoe asked.

"It was so important for Edna to get every detail right, especially on our opening weekend. Sometimes she'd wake me in the middle of the night because she suddenly remembered something she needed to put in the rooms before you—" he looked at Lauren "—and the other ladies arrived."

"My room – suite – was beautiful," Lauren told him. "I loved the lavender shower gel."

"See?" Harry beamed. "Edna was good at things like that. Me, I can do handy work and gardening and I enjoy talking to people, but Edna was the one with all the drive." His face suddenly crumpled. "What am I going to do here all alone?"

"You could operate the B&B yourself," Zoe suggested.

"I don't know." Harry sounded doubtful.

"Do you need to do anything right now?" Lauren asked gently. "I thought you were retired."

"That's true." He brightened a little. "I'll still get my pension, and we were able to buy this place outright. I should be able to afford to stay here without renting out the rooms."

They spoke to him for a while longer, then Harry invited them – and Annie – to take a walk in the garden before they left.

"Your cat might like to see it," he told them.

Annie sniffed the grass, tried to chase a butterfly while towing Lauren along, and investigated the flowers, Lauren making sure they only looked at the blooms that were safe for cats.

"This is a beautiful place." Zoe stretched out her arms and whirled around. "Can you imagine living here? No neighbors, just peace and quiet."

A bird suddenly chirped a pretty tune, causing Zoe to smile.

"You don't think you'd get lonely by yourself here?" Lauren asked.

"No." Zoe shook her head. "Not if I had Chris – or you and Annie," she added hastily.

"I understand," Lauren replied. And she did.

"This would be a great place for a honeymoon," Zoe mused.

Not if Edna disturbed you every five minutes. Lauren was instantly ashamed of herself. The poor woman had been murdered, and Harry truly seemed to have loved her.

They said goodbye to Harry when they were ready to leave.

"Your fellow Mitch doesn't have any inside information on the investigation, does he?" Harry asked as he accompanied them to their car.

"No," Lauren replied. "He's off the case, anyway."

"Too bad." Harry shook his head. "Detective Castern has been pretty brusque with me. All he's told me is he's pursuing every possible lead. Whatever that means."

"I *am* sorry," Lauren told him.

"Me, too," Zoe added.

"Brrt."

They waved goodbye to him as they drove away. Lauren wished she could have shared some details with him on the search for Edna's killer, but she didn't have any. Did Harry's request for inside information mean he was innocent? Or guilty?

CHAPTER 12

"What are we going to do today?" Zoe asked the next morning at breakfast. She slathered butter on a piece of whole wheat toast.

"The usual, I guess," Lauren told her. "Grocery shopping, and checking on Mrs. Finch." Tomorrow, Tuesday, they would open the café as usual at nine-thirty.

"Brrt," Annie seemed to agree, her ears pricking up at the mention of their friend.

"Ooh, and gnome thief spotting." Zoe grabbed her phone and checked the live camera feed. When they had arrived home yesterday from visiting Harry, they'd checked that the gnome was still in the garden.

"I wonder when the thief is going to steal our gnome." Zoe crunched into her toast.

"Maybe he won't," Lauren suggested. "Maybe he has enough gnomes and doesn't need to steal anymore."

"Is that what Mitch said?" Zoe furrowed her brow. "I know he called you last night."

"Yes, he did," Lauren replied. "And I know Chris called you."

"Yeah." A dreamy expression flitted across Zoe's face for an instant. "So, did Mitch mention anything about the gnome thief?" She was back to business.

"Only that there haven't been any more thefts reported," Lauren replied.

"Huh." Zoe's eyebrows drew together, then she looked down at the phone, her eyes widening. "Lauren!"

"What?"

"Look!" She tapped the screen.

Lauren peered at the device. A figure dressed in black crept through the backyard.

"Brrt?" Annie stared at the screen, then jumped off the kitchen chair, running to the back door. "Brrt!"

"We have to call Mitch." Lauren grabbed her phone from her pocket and speed dialed him.

"There's no time for that." Zoe ran to the back door, unbolting it. "Let's go!"

"Zoe!" But Lauren called out to thin air. Zoe and Annie had raced out into the garden.

"Stop!" she heard Zoe yell.

She ran after them, holding the phone to her ear. Voicemail. Breathlessly, she rapped out a message for Mitch, then shoved the phone into the pocket of her capris.

The figure continued to creep along the side of the garden, heading toward the gnome.

"Got you!" Zoe charged like an Amazon warrior as she sped toward the thief, Annie by her side.

"Wha—" the figure tottered and spun around, only their eyes showing as the rest of their face was covered in a balaclava.

Lauren briefly wondered if the thief was getting hot in his – or her – outfit. The day was already warm and the sun shone from the cloudless blue sky. Her eyes narrowed. Now she was nearer, the criminal's figure seemed a little hunched. She glanced down. Black orthopedic shoes.

She had a sudden inkling she knew who the thief might be – although she could hardly believe it. Maybe she was wrong?

"We've got you on camera!" Zoe pulled off the balaclava.

"Ow!" Martha patted her gray curls back into place, frowning at Zoe.

Zoe's mouth hung open.

"Hi, Martha," Lauren greeted her. She'd been right.

"Brrt!"

"Huh?" Zoe continued to gape at the senior.

"Where's your walker?" Lauren asked her.

"Around the corner." Martha pointed down the lawn towards the side gate with a trembling finger. "Do you think you could get it for me? I need to sit down."

Lauren fetched the walker. "Here you go."

"Thanks." Martha sank down on the black vinyl seat.

"But – how – what?" Zoe shook her head.

"Why were you trying to steal our gnome?" Lauren asked.

"Because – because—" Martha looked miserable.

"Did you steal everyone's gnomes?" Zoe got her brain back.

"Of course not!" Martha sounded shocked. "We took turns."

"Turns?" Lauren asked.

"Brrt?"

"We?" Zoe added.

"See, one of my friends is housebound," Martha explained, pulling at her black turtleneck sweater. "I didn't realize I'd get so hot in this get up," she mumbled.

The three of them waited for her to continue her explanation. Zoe folded her arms.

"Okay, okay. My friends and I at the senior center all decided to steal a gnome each for our friend. She used to have gnomes in her garden growing up and she told me a little while ago how she'd love to have gnomes in her garden again. She loved gardening but now she's in a wheelchair most of the time and can only look at the yard, not work in it."

"With you so far," Zoe said.

"So we all decided to get her some gnomes. But do you know how much they cost?"

"No." Lauren shook her head.

"Thirty dollars if you're lucky. Sometimes more. Plus shipping if you order online because you can't get out to a garden center." Martha tsked. "We're all on fixed incomes. Then someone said one of their neighbors had a gnome in the corner of their garden for years and it was pretty dirty, and they didn't think they would miss it. So we hatched a plan to rescue neglected gnomes." She sat back on the walker seat, looking a little pleased with herself.

"It's still stealing," Lauren pointed out. "People did miss their gnomes because they reported the thefts to the police."

"Brrt," Annie scolded Martha.

"I know." Martha looked down at the feline. "Don't look at me like that, Annie. I know it was wrong, but it seemed harmless. And we wanted to help an old lady – older than me – to feel better."

"Did she know what you were doing?" Zoe asked.

"No." Martha shook her head. "She would be shocked, I'm sure, and refuse the gnomes when we brought them all over to her house. We haven't done that yet. We were going to tell her that members from the senior center had donated gnomes they didn't want any more. Well, it was *nearly* the truth."

"Maybe the people you stole from would have donated the gnomes if you had asked them," Lauren felt compelled to point out.

"We didn't think of that," Martha admitted in a small voice. "It was fun planning the heists. I was the one in charge."

"Why doesn't that surprise me?" Lauren shook her head.

"But why did you decide to steal our gnome on a Monday morning?" Zoe asked curiously.

"Everyone knows you go grocery shopping and visit Mrs. Finch today," Martha explained. "I thought you would have left the house by now."

"Are we really that predictable?" Zoe asked.

"Brrt." *Yes.*

"Are you going to arrest me?" Martha held out her wrists as if expecting one of them to slap handcuffs on her.

Lauren and Zoe looked at each other.

"I called Mitch and left a message for him," Lauren told her.

"And there are cameras." Zoe pointed to the back of the house and the old shed that housed the lawnmower.

"When did you have cameras put in?" Martha's eyes widened. "Is that why you put a gnome in the garden and told me about it? You're running a sting operation!" She straightened her spine.

"We thought you might tell your friends about our gnome and word would get around. But we didn't think you were involved in the thefts," Lauren explained.

"Yeah!"

"Brrt!"

"I'm sorry, Martha." Lauren had mixed feelings about the sting operation now she knew who the thief was.

"Maybe Mitch won't arrest you," Zoe suggested. "Tell him what you told us."

"Yes," Lauren added, an idea taking shape, "maybe if you all apologize to the people you took the gnomes from and returned them, they might decide not to press charges."

"I knew you girls were my friends." Martha brightened up. "You too, Annie." She glanced down at the tabby, who sat next to the walker.

"Brrt!" Annie agreed.

Lauren's phone rang.

"It's Mitch." She glanced at the screen and accepted the call. Briefly telling him what had transpired, she was glad to hear him chuckle at the mention of Martha.

"He'll be here in a moment," Lauren told them after ending the call. "He said to stay right where we are."

Mitch arrived a few minutes later. Zoe was telling Martha about the ice cream place Chris had taken her to in Sacramento when Mitch strode into the garden.

"You'd better tell me what's going on with these gnomes, Martha." His expression was serious.

Martha repeated her reasons for stealing the garden ornaments. When she'd finished, Mitch shook his head.

"I haven't heard anything like that before." A slight smile edge the corner of his mouth.

"Does that mean I can go?" Martha asked hopefully.

"No. Sorry. I'll have to take you down to the station. And you'll need to give me the names of your co-conspirators."

"But I'm not a snitch!" Martha's mouth parted in shock.

"I already know they visit the senior center. If you don't co-operate, I'll go down there and question every member – as well as the employees. One of them is bound to crack." Now he was in full-on cop mode.

"Okay, okay." Martha crumbled. "I hope they won't be mad at me for telling on them."

Lauren's heart went out to the elderly woman. Yes, what she had done was wrong, but it had been for a good reason.

"Mitch, can I speak to you for a second?" She walked a few steps away from the group.

"Are you okay?" He joined her.

"I'm fine. But you're not going to arrest Martha, are you?"

"I hope not. But I need to do this by the book."

"What if the gnome owners don't want to press charges?" Lauren asked hopefully.

"That's a possibility. I don't want Martha to have a criminal record or go through the court process, but I do need to take her down to the station. Don't worry, I'll make sure she gets a cup of coffee or juice or whatever she likes to drink, and I'll be the one questioning her."

"She likes hot chocolate with lots of marshmallows," Lauren informed him. "But maybe not today – she said she was getting very warm in her outfit."

"I'll see what I can do." He smiled at her reassuringly. "I'll stop by later today and update you."

Lauren watched Mitch gently lead Martha out of the garden.

"Phew." Zoe fanned herself. "Mitch is impressive when he's in cop mode."

"I think he's impressive all the time." Lauren admitted, blushing.

"That's what I think about Chris." Zoe giggled. "Wait until we tell Mrs. Finch who the gnome thief turned out to be!"

"One of them, at any rate."

"Brrt!"

***

After visiting Mrs. Finch, and telling her the news about Martha, they took Annie home. Then they went to the supermarket.

"Look!" Lauren eyed a furry mouse toy with a squeaker. She hadn't bought Annie a new toy for a couple of months.

"Annie definitely needs that!" Zoe grabbed it off the shelf and put it in the cart.

As they browsed the aisles, Lauren thought about what she needed to make a new cupcake creation. She'd finally decided on raspberry bonus cupcakes – a vanilla cupcake hiding a hidden raspberry in the middle of the batter, with pretty pale pink frosting decorated with fresh raspberries, strawberries, and blueberries.

Later that day, she mixed up the cake batter, Annie 'supervising' by sitting at the table and watching, occasionally adding sound effects by making her toy mouse squeak. Zoe had disappeared into the living room, saying she was going to work out how many more pottery mugs she needed to make based on her current sales of five.

The doorbell rang just as she was mixing the flour in with a spatula.

"I'll get it," Zoe called out.

A minute later, two sets of footsteps sounded down the hall.

"It's Mitch," Zoe said unnecessarily as both of them stood in the kitchen doorway.

"Hi." Lauren smiled at him.

He returned her smile. He looked cool and fresh in fawn slacks and a dove gray shirt.

"Brrt!" Annie dangled her mouse in her mouth, looking up at Mitch. Then she dropped the toy and stepped on it with her paw.

Squeak!

"Is that a new toy, Annie?" Mitch's eyes crinkled at the corners.

"Brrt!" *Yes!*

"I bought it for her today," Lauren said.

"I thought I bought it for her!" Zoe giggled, then she sobered. "What's happening with Martha?"

"She's given a full confession," Mitch replied. "I contacted the gnome owners and once I explained everything, none of them wanted to press charges. Martha will apologize personally to them, and that should be the end of the matter."

"That's good," Lauren said with relief.

"What about the gnomes?" Zoe asked.

"Brrt?" Annie added.

"What about them?" Mitch frowned.

"Will the owners keep them or will they donate them to Martha's friend? So she can enjoy them in her garden," Zoe explained.

"As far as I know, the owners are going to keep them for themselves," Mitch replied.

"Huh." Zoe looked deep in thought as she wandered down the hall.

"Oh, I should tell you." Lauren suddenly remembered. "Zoe and I thought it would be fun if we double dated on Sunday –if you're free. We want to go to the farmers' market again and there's an amazing ice cream place Zoe told me about. Chris took her there on Saturday."

"Sounds good." He smiled. "Why not?"

"Brrt?" *Me too?* Annie asked hopefully.

"Oh, Annie, the farmers' market doesn't allow pets," Lauren said regretfully. She'd already looked at the website to check.

"Brrp." Annie jutted out her lower lip in a pout.

"Maybe you could have another video play date with AJ," Lauren suggested.

"Brrp." Annie looked happier.

***

The next day, Lauren got up a little earlier. She wanted to mix up the batter for her new raspberry bonus cupcakes and have the first ones ready by the time they opened the café at nine-thirty.

Crunch, crunch, crunch.

In the kitchen, Zoe waved goodbye as she munched on her buttery toast. Annie followed Lauren down the private hallway into the café.

"We might even beat Ed this morning," she told her.

"Brrt!"

Annie sat in her cat bed while Lauren had the gleaming commercial kitchen to herself. The new cupcakes had been a hit with Zoe last night, and Lauren had found it hard to stop after eating just one.

Annie had looked with approval as she'd watched Lauren decorate the cakes with pale pink frosting and summer berries.

Now, Lauren wanted to recreate yesterday's cupcake magic.

The first batch were in the oven by the time Ed stomped into the kitchen.

"Hi Ed," she greeted the burly baker.

"Oh – hi, Lauren." He seemed a little surprised to see her this early in the morning.

"I've got a new cupcake for you to try – I'll set one aside for you."

"Thanks." He smiled briefly.

She entered the café space. Zoe unstacked chairs while Annie 'supervised' from her cat bed.

"The raspberry bonus cupcakes are in the oven," she told her cousin.

"Awesome." Zoe grinned.

They chatted about their upcoming double date on Sunday for a few minutes, then concentrated on getting the café ready before the cupcakes were cool enough for Lauren to frost.

Lauren poured a brand-new bag of coffee beans into the hopper – it was one of her customers' favorites, living up to its promise of tasting like hazelnut, chocolate, and spices.

"I wonder if we'll get lots of people coming in today," Zoe mused as she unbolted the big oak and glass door right on the dot of nine-thirty.

"I hope so," Lauren replied. She wanted to know if her cupcake creation would be a hit – or a flop.

"Hi!" A few minutes later, Claire pushed a stroller into the shop.

"Annie!" A blonde toddler waved a chubby hand in the feline's direction.

"Hi Claire, hi, Molly." Lauren smiled at the sight of two of her favorite customers. She knew little Molly was one of Annie's favorites as well.

"Brrt!" Annie ran to greet the mother daughter duo.

"Where should we sit, Annie?" Claire asked.

"Brrt." *Right this way.* Annie led them to a four-seater near the counter.

"What can we get you?" Lauren and Zoe approached their friends.

"Lauren has a new cupcake flavor for you to try." Zoe was her biggest cheerleader. "I tried a test batch last night and they were delicious."

"Then you must give me one." Claire smiled at them. Her outfit of shorts and a green t-shirt suited her athletic figure. "And Molly would love a babycino, wouldn't you, darling?"

"Cino!" Molly agreed, gently giving Annie 'fairy pats' on her furry shoulder.

"And I'll have a large latte, please," Claire continued. "Do you have a minute to sit and chat?"

"Of course." Lauren sat down. So did Zoe.

By tacit understanding Lauren and Zoe didn't mention Martha's escapades yesterday. Instead, they spoke about their upcoming double date, Zoe filling in

Claire on the ice cream shop in Sacramento. "I bet Molly would enjoy going there." She winked at the toddler.

"I bet she would," Claire agreed. "So would I. Maybe Molly and I could surprise my husband for lunch one day."

"Icweam?" Molly's eyes widened.

"A special treat for lunch one day," Claire told her. "A treat for daddy, too."

"Tweat!" Molly beamed, her eyes round and sparkling.

"I guess we'd better get your babycino treat right now." Lauren rose.

"I'll bring over your cupcake," Zoe promised, following Lauren back to the counter.

Lauren ground the beans and steamed the milk for the beverages.

"I feel like sinking my teeth into this cupcake right now." Zoe stared longingly at the cake, pale pink frosting piled high in a decorative swirl, dotted with fresh raspberries, strawberries, and blueberries.

"Me too," Lauren admitted ruefully. She'd continue to keep her curves if she indulged too often in her own baking – and Ed's pastries.

"I'll put away one for each for us." Zoe placed two into a cardboard box and tucked them under the counter.

"Thanks." Lauren hoped the rest of the batch would sell, mainly so she wouldn't be tempted to eat more than one today.

They brought the drinks and sweet treat over to Claire and Molly.

"Annie!" Molly pointed to her espresso cup filled with warm steamed milk and dusted with chocolate powder, tiny pink and white marshmallows dotting the surface.

"Brrt." Annie's eyes sparkled as she looked at the little girl's babycino.

"I love your latte art," Claire told them as she accepted the mug. Lauren had created a swan on top of the micro foam.

"Thanks." Lauren smiled.

Claire's eyes lit up in anticipation as Zoe placed the cupcake in front of her. "I also love raspberries, strawberries, and blueberries."

"Let me know what you think." Lauren was a little anxious as Claire forked up a small amount. Apart from Zoe and herself, she was the first person to have tried her new creation. Mitch had to return to work yesterday before the test batch of cupcakes were in the oven.

Claire chewed, swallowed – and beamed. "I love it. The frosting isn't too sweet, but it adds just the right touch to the cake crumb – and I love all the fresh fruit on top plus the raspberry hiding inside."

"I'm glad you like it." Lauren beamed.

"These are going to be our next big hit," Zoe predicted.

"I hope so," Lauren replied.

"Brrt!"

***

When Ed returned from his lunchbreak, he told Lauren how much he'd enjoyed his cupcake sample. Coming from Ed, that was high praise.

"Thanks." Lauren smiled. "Is it okay with you if Annie and AJ have another video play date on Sunday?" She explained about her and Zoe's upcoming double date.

"Sure thing," he replied. "I'll make certain AJ can reach the phone easily."

He then told her he was thinking up a new idea for his Danish pastries. "I'll experiment at home first, though."

"I'd love to hear more about it when you're ready," she replied. His last creation had been honeyed walnut Danishes, which seemed to be the most popular of all his pastries. Customers had admitted that sometimes they came to the café just to snag a honeyed walnut – and to see Annie, of course.

"Look who's here!" Zoe greeted her when she returned to the café. Lauren followed Zoe's tilt of her head.

Donna and her sister Barbara, the winners of the bed and breakfast competition, sat at a table near the back.

"Have they ordered?"

"Not yet," Zoe replied.

Lauren scanned the café. Annie sat primly in her basket, her new squeaky toy partly hiding beneath her blanket. Since it was after the lunch rush, there were only a few customers sitting at tables, including the sisters.

"I wonder why they're here." Lauren crinkled her brow.

"I know," Zoe agreed. "I mean, yes, we do have awesome coffee and cakes and pastries – probably the best they'll get in or out of Sacramento—"

"Zoe!" Lauren didn't know whether to laugh or not at Zoe's pride in their offerings.

"—but it is an hour out of their way if they just wanted to enjoy a latte and something to eat."

"Maybe they wanted to see Annie again," Lauren suggested.

"That's true," Zoe mused. "But I don't think they wanted her to sit with them, because after she showed them to that table, she stayed with them for a couple of minutes, and then strolled back to her basket. She didn't show them her new toy mouse, either."

"Should we go over there?" Lauren asked.

"Why not?" Zoe's dark brown eyes flickered with curiosity. "Not much else has happened today, apart from Claire and Molly coming in."

They headed over to the sisters' table.

"Are you ready to order?" Zoe whipped out a notepad from the pocket of her cargo pants.

"Oh, I thought we had to order at the counter," Donna said.

"That's true," Lauren replied. "But it's quiet at the moment."

"We thought you might need help deciding," Zoe told them. "So it's the perfect opportunity to tell you about Lauren's new raspberry bonus cupcakes."

Zoe sounded so enthusiastic about the new offering that Lauren didn't like to ask her to stop. By the time she had finished though, both sisters had ordered the treat, plus a cappuccino each.

"Be right back," Zoe promised, as they threaded their way back to the counter.

As Lauren ground the beans, the machine whirring and grinding, Zoe frowned. "We didn't find out anything," she muttered.

"Maybe that's because you didn't ask them anything about – you know," Lauren murmured.

"But I did sell them cupcakes," Zoe pointed out.

Zoe plated the treats while Lauren made the cappuccinos, designing a peacock for one of them and a swan for the other.

"I bet they don't get latte art like that in Sacramento," Zoe said in satisfaction as she peered at the mugs.

"Unless they went to Amy's café," Lauren reminded her. That was where they had taken the advanced latte art course last year.

As soon as they brought over the order, Zoe started.

"We visited Harry at his bed and breakfast in Zeke's Ridge on the weekend," she said conversationally as she placed a cupcake before each sister.

"Really?" Barbara widened her eyes. "How is he?"

"He seemed such a nice man." Donna nodded.

"Devastated," Zoe replied. "It's such a shame what happened to his wife."

"Did you know her – or Harry?" Donna asked.

"No." Zoe shook her head. "We took Annie with us, though, and Harry invited us to stroll in the garden."

"Annie enjoyed it." Lauren glanced over at the feline, still sitting in her basket, her ears pricked as if she knew they were talking about her.

"I also loved the foyer. It was furnished so beautifully," Zoe told them. "We saw the guest register you guys wrote in – Lauren and Mitch, did too. Although I did have problems reading your last names." She giggled.

"Edna was most insistent we fill in our details," Barbara said. "Still, I suppose she needed to do things properly."

"She seemed very excited about their opening weekend." Donna gave a little nod.

"I entered the competition just like Lauren and you guys, but unfortunately I didn't win. I wish I had, though – apart from what happened. All that Victorian architecture, all brought back to life."

"Just like here." Donna surveyed the café's pale yellow walls and pine chairs and tables. "There seems to be a lot of Victoriana in this town."

"Just like Lauren's cottage," Zoe told them.

"But it's certainly not on the scale of Harry and Edna's B&B," Lauren hastened to add.

"Still, I'd love to live in something with real character," Donna said wistfully. She glanced at her sister. "Not that I don't enjoy modern living as well."

Barbara laughed. "You both moved in with me knowing it was a modern box."

"I had to sell my house." Donna sounded downcast. "It was a Craftsman. A real beauty."

"That's too bad," Zoe said, real sympathy in her voice.

"Still." Barbara patted her sister's hand. "I'm sure things will start to look up for you."

Lauren and Zoe headed back to the counter. None of the other customers seemed to need their attention.

"Huh," Zoe said thoughtfully.

"What does that mean?"

"I don't think we learned anything at all."

"What were you hoping for?" Lauren asked.

"Let's see." Zoe started counting off her fingers. "If it wasn't an intruder, then someone staying at the B&B that night killed Edna. Not you – or Mitch, of course," she added hastily as she noticed Lauren's expression. "So that leaves Harry, Donna, and Barbara."

"But why would Harry kill his wife?" Lauren asked. "You met him on Sunday – he really seemed to have loved her."

"I know." Zoe nodded.

"Do you really think it was Donna or Barbara?" Lauren kept her voice low as she glanced at the sisters' table. They seemed nice enough women.

"What do we really know about them?" Zoe posed the question.

"Nothing," Lauren replied after a moment. "Except they live in Sacramento."

"And Donna has moved in with her sister for some reason."

"And sold her house," Lauren added. "Do we even know what Donna does for a living?"

"Huh." Zoe drew her eyebrows together. "No, I don't think she mentioned what her job actually was when they visited the café last time."

"Hmm." Now it was Lauren's turn to ponder that information – or lack of it.

"So who else was there at the B&B at the time of the murder? No one, that's who!" Zoe proclaimed.

"So no one did it?" Lauren quizzed her.

"It must be someone we don't know about, if it's not the two sisters or Harry," Zoe said. She sounded so sure.

"How are we going to find someone we don't know about? And why would they kill Edna?"

"Maybe the restaurant owners in Zeke's Ridge got together and killed her because she was annoying them," Zoe suggested. "The server at the Italian restaurant told you Edna annoyed the manager there."

"That's true. But I can't imagine that scenario happening – can you?" She eyed Zoe.

"Not really," Zoe admitted.

"I just hope Detective Castern has better leads than we do," Lauren said. "I don't want him returning and questioning me again."

"And we don't want Mitch stuck on gnome detail forever," Zoe added. "Although that's resolved now."

"I wonder who the woman is, who's housebound and wanted gnomes in her garden," Lauren murmured.

"I'm sure Martha will tell us," Zoe replied. "Hey, I meant to ask you, do you want to buy a gnome for Martha's friend? I'm going to. If we buy one each we can split the shipping." Zoe gestured to the tip jar on the counter, silver coins and dollar bills cramming it full. "I already counted it this morning. My half is twenty dollars." She shared the tips with Ed.

"That's nearly enough to buy a gnome," Lauren remarked.

"According to Martha." Zoe grinned.

"Why not?" Lauren agreed. She could afford to buy one for Martha's friend. She just wished she'd thought of it earlier.

"I'll order them right now!" Zoe whipped out her phone from her pocket and showed Lauren the screen. "See, I've already been looking at them."

Lauren found it difficult to make up her mind between a gnome wearing green trousers and a blue jacket, and one wearing navy trousers and a red jacket.

"Brrt?" Annie wandered over to them, tilting her head as she stared up at them.

"Which gnome do you think I should buy?" Lauren came around the side of the counter, bent down, and showed Annie the screen. "It's for Martha's friend."

"She wants gnome statues in her garden," Zoe added. "To cheer her up."

"Brrt." Annie delicately placed her paw on the screen, right on top of the gnome wearing navy trousers and a red jacket.

"Thank you." Lauren smiled, adding that particular gnome to the shopping cart. "Annie thinks this is the one." Lauren handed Zoe the phone.

"Would you like to choose another one, Annie?" Zoe leaned over the counter and handed the phone back to Lauren. "I can't decide, either."

"Brrt." Annie's mouth tilted up at the corners. She peered at the screen, and once again delicately placed her paw on the screen.

Lauren looked at Annie's choice.

"Purple trousers and a yellow jacket," she told Zoe.

"That's because Annie knows I like purple." She winked at the cat.

"Brrt!"

Zoe ordered the two statues. "Is it bad that I know my credit card number off by heart, including the little code on the back of it?" she asked as she tapped away on her phone.

"No?" Lauren replied, guilty of the same crime.

"There," Zoe said in satisfaction. "All ordered. It should arrive in a couple of days. I can't wait to tell Martha."

"Tell me what?" Martha barreled into the café, pushing her walker. "I've just been sprung from the big house!"

CHAPTER 13

At Martha's dramatic announcement, they peppered her with questions, Martha admitting that she'd left the police station yesterday and gone home.

"I think I definitely need a hot chocolate right now, though." She sank down at the four-seater table Annie had shown her, sitting on Martha's walker seat as the senior wheeled them toward that particular table.

"With lots of marshmallows?" Zoe grinned.

"You betcha."

Annie sat at the table with Martha.

"Do you think she needs a cupcake?" Lauren whispered to her cousin.

"Definitely," Zoe agreed.

Lauren plated a raspberry bonus cupcake and brought it over to Martha.

"On the house."

"Thanks." Martha's eyes lit up at the raspberries, strawberries, and blueberries decorating the pale pink frosting. "You girls are good to me. So was Mitch."

"He was?" Lauren sat down for a second. She'd left Zoe cramming a ton of marshmallows into the cocoa-laced foam.

"He gave me a cup of coffee and chocolate chip cookies," Martha mumbled around a mouthful of frosting.

"I'm glad." Lauren smiled.

"The coffee wasn't nearly as good as yours," Martha told her. "You know what police coffee is like."

Lauren didn't, actually.

"But he's a good one all right," Martha told her. "You hold onto him." She pointed her frosting-laden fork at Lauren.

"I will," Lauren promised. *I hope I will.*

"So of course I had to tell Mitch all about my gnome operation," Martha continued. "And he said he understood. So this morning I went around and apologized to everyone who had a gnome taken, because it was my idea, and Mitch said he'd make sure my friends will apologize to the people they appropriated a gnome from."

"Here's your hot chocolate." Zoe brought over a large mug crammed full of pink and white marshmallows.

"You're the best." Martha beamed at her. "You too, Annie. And Lauren, of course," she added hastily.

As Martha drank her hot chocolate, Annie's attention was drawn to the entrance door.

"Brrt!"

Lauren turned around.

"Mitch!" She hurried to greet him, Annie by her side.

"Brrt?" Annie tilted her head as she looked up at him.

"I think Annie wants to know if you'd like to join us at Martha's table." Lauren smiled at him.

"Why not? I've got a few minutes." He returned her smile, looking cool and unrumpled even though it was quite warm outside.

"I've just told Martha that Lauren and I ordered a gnome each for her friend who's housebound," Zoe told them when they reached the table.

"At least she'll have two gnomes to look at," Martha said. "I know! I can ask my friends if they want to buy a gnome with me. There are six of us so that might only cost us seven dollars each or less with shipping if we pool our money together."

"Would these be the same friends you committed the crimes with?" There was a touch of sternness in Mitch's voice.

"Yep. I've contacted them and explained why I ratted on them. They said they understood."

"I think that's a good idea, then." He nodded.

"So that's three gnomes," Zoe said in satisfaction.

"Four." Mitch smiled slightly. "I've already asked the department and they said we can donate the one used in the sting operation."

"You *are* a good one." Martha beamed at him.

Lauren noticed a faint flush of crimson on his cheeks.

"Brrt!"

***

Lauren and Zoe started cleaning up at the dot of five o'clock. Their last customer had left a few minutes ago.

"What should we do tonight?" Zoe asked them as she started stacking chairs on tables.

"Have dinner and watch TV, I suppose. Or is that too predictable?" Lauren remembered Martha's comment from the day before when they'd caught her attempting to steal the gnome.

"After today, I wouldn't mind putting my feet up and watching something good," Zoe admitted.

"It turned out to be busy, after all." Lauren smiled as she thought of the day's takings. After Mitch had come in, there'd been a steady stream of customers.

The sound of the entrance door opening caught her attention and she swung around.

"I forgot to lock it," she murmured.

"It's Donna." Zoe placed another chair on the table and hurried to greet her. "We're closed now. Sorry."

"Did you forget something?" Lauren came over. Sometimes Annie discovered something left behind by a customer, which they called Annie's Lost and Found, but the feline hadn't alerted them that she'd unearthed anything unusual today. Apart from occasionally moving her squeaky toy around the café, although she'd resisted the temptation to make it squeak.

"Yes," Donna replied. "I need one of your pottery mugs, Zoe. I meant to buy one earlier today but I forgot." She shook her head. "I don't know what's wrong with me."

"Sure!" Zoe rushed to the counter. "I can put it in a paper bag for you. That will be fifteen dollars."

"I think they're very cute," Donna continued. "And Annie's portrait is beautiful – just like she is."

"Brrt," Annie seemed to agree, standing near the counter.

"Thanks." Zoe rang up the sale on the cash register.

"Zoe," Lauren said in a warning tone. There had been something niggling away at the back of her mind since Donna and her sister had visited earlier that day, and now that Donna had returned, she thought she knew what it was.

"It's okay, we haven't closed the register yet," Zoe told her.

Donna opened her purse. But instead of pulling out her wallet, she pulled out a gun.

"Eek!" Zoe's eyes widened.

"You killed Edna," Lauren said in shocked awe.

"Come behind the register." Donna waved the gun in Lauren's direction. "The cat, too."

"Her name is Annie," Lauren told her.

"Brrt?" Annie's green eyes rounded as she stared at the three humans.

"We'd better do what she says," Lauren told her, scooping her up and hugging her close. Her heart pounded as she joined Zoe behind the counter.

Donna's mouth tightened as she surveyed the three of them down the barrel of the gun.

"I probably didn't have to do this," she muttered. "I thought you two had figured it out, but I don't think you did."

"Figured what out?" Zoe tapped her cheek.

"She's not a widow," Lauren told her.

"She's not?" Zoe scrunched her nose.

"Two clues. You missed two clues and didn't even know it. Gah!" Donna shook her head in disgust.

"The guest register," Lauren said slowly. "You said that night we were all at the B&B that you were a widow."

"And Edna made me write in that stupid book," Donna remarked. "Then you, Zoe, told me right here, today, that you'd read the names in the guest book. I thought you were letting me know you knew I was the killer when you said you had problems reading my handwriting. Like a test to see if I would react. I wrote my name as messily as I could in that guest book so it wouldn't be legible, even though I used my sister's last name instead of my own."

"But didn't Barbara want to know why you used a different surname in the guest register?" Lauren asked.

"I told my sister I didn't think it was any of Edna's business what my last name was, or if I was married." Donna shrugged. "I'm a pretty private person, so it wasn't much of a surprise to Barbara that I did something like that."

"And the other clue was when Barbara said today that you *both* were living with her," Lauren said.

"Very good," Donna said in grudging approval. "Maybe *you're* not too stupid to live, after all."

"I'm guessing you didn't really want one of my pottery mugs," Zoe said sadly.

"That's right." Donna nodded. "They're not bad for an amateur, but they've got a bulge near the handle. Although, I must admit that your portrait of Annie isn't half bad."

"Thanks – I think," Zoe muttered.

"Brrt?" Annie asked softly. She was still scooped against Lauren's chest, her muscles tensing, as if bracing for action.

"Don't worry about your cat. My sister can't stop talking about how pretty she is. I'll take her home with me, and tell Barbara the police insisted I give her a good home."

"So Barbara doesn't know anything about this?" Zoe guessed.

"No. And it's going to stay that way."

"Why did you kill Edna?" Lauren asked softly.

"She had my husband fired." Donna scowled, the gun wobbling in her hand. "He was a high school principal and she caught him doing something that technically he shouldn't be doing."

"What?" Zoe asked.

"He took some pens home to save money."

"That's all?" Zoe frowned.

"It's still stealing," Lauren reminded her.

"Yes, it is, but how many people do something like that? A lot, let me tell you."

Lauren thought of Martha, who'd defended her plan to steal gnomes because she'd wanted to cheer up her friend.

"He got fired for stealing pens?" Zoe queried.

"Yes. The board wanted to let it go, and just give him a warning but Edna made such a big fuss about it, that in the end, they had no choice but to fire him."

"I'm sorry," Lauren offered.

"Me too," Zoe added.

"Brrt."

"But Edna had an ulterior motive. She wanted a full-time position at the school, but none of the teachers liked her. Neither did my husband."

"How come?" Zoe asked.

"Because she was a bit nosey?" Lauren guessed.

"Yes. A real busybody. She got into everyone's business. How do you think she knew my husband took some pens home? Because she spied on him. Just like she spied on everyone else. My husband said he used to hear the kids groaning down the hall when they walked into class and saw Edna substituting. So when a full-time position came up, Edna applied for it but my husband didn't grant her the position. That's why she reported him for stealing."

"What happened after she got your husband fired?" Lauren asked, intrigued despite herself.

"She still didn't get the full-time position," Donna said in remembered satisfaction. "Ha ha!" The gun shook slightly. "And the last we heard was that she retired not long after."

"So the first time you saw her after that was at the B&B?" Zoe asked.

"Yes. It was actually the first time I'd met her but I knew it was her for sure when she made that crack about my messy handwriting. I knew all about her from my husband, including what she looked like, how she acted, and what her husband used to do for a living. Edna loved talking about herself when she was at the school. After the stolen pen incident, my husband couldn't stop complaining about what had happened. I heard about Edna *every day.* So I knew it was the right woman.

"I couldn't believe it when we arrived at the B&B and met Edna and Harry. That morning before we left Sacramento my husband had been complaining again about how Edna had ruined his life, and there she was, in the flesh! I was confident she wouldn't know who I was because my husband isn't one to talk about his family to work colleagues, and he's not a soppy sort of man who would have a photo of me on his desk." She sounded as if she wished her husband *was* that type of man.

"Barbara won the weekend at the B&B and invited me so we could have a break from our husbands and have some fun. Luckily I didn't enter the contest myself or Edna might have recognized my surname, although I don't know how they picked the winners. Maybe they tossed all the entries into a bag, closed their eyes and picked out two envelopes?" Donna shook herself. "Anyway, I couldn't pass up this opportunity to even the score with Edna."

"Stealing pens and killing someone are two totally different crimes," Zoe observed.

"Yes, they are," Donna replied. "But Edna ruined my life – and my husband's. He wasn't able to get another job as a principal – or even as a teacher. The pen incident branded him a thief on his school file and no other schools will take him. He had to get a job as a dog groomer after doing a training course, and I have to work as a greeter in a department store. Do you know how tired my feet are at the end of a shift?"

"I can guess," Lauren replied softly. Sometimes her feet ached by the time they closed at five, and she and Zoe had stools behind the counter they could sit on for a few minutes during the day.

"I didn't have to work before," Donna replied. "Now I have to make my lunch – and my husband's – and go to work and pin a big cheery smile on my face as I greet customers. And, the reason we're now living with my sister and her husband is we lost our house."

"How come?" Zoe asked.

"Because we couldn't afford to pay the mortgage any longer now my husband was out of work. Even with both our new jobs, we can't afford to make the repayments. And it's not only that." She sighed, lowering the gun for a second before realizing what she'd just done and raising it again. "I didn't realize how over-extended we were. We were able to make our monthly payments for our cars and credit cards, and the house while my husband was school principal but now …"

"It's all come tumbling down?" Lauren guessed.

"Exactly. And it's all Edna's fault." Donna stiffened her spine and glared at them. "I don't know how we'll ever buy another house again. We have no money and we still have to make our monthly payments on our cars and credit cards."

"But if you bought the house a while ago, wouldn't you have some equity left in it after you paid back the bank?" Zoe asked.

"Not when you have a second mortgage – and a third," Donna admitted. "I had no choice. Don't you see that?"

"But how did you kill her?" Lauren asked. "I haven't heard that the police found the weapon."

"An old silver candlestick that was in our room – no, suite, Edna called it, didn't she? Of course, I was very careful to wipe my fingerprints off it." She laughed. "It was so easy. After I hit her with it, I ran down the stairs, swapped it for an identical candlestick in the foyer, wiped my prints using the velvet drapes in there, then returned the foyer candlestick to my room."

"But how did you do it without anyone seeing you?" Lauren asked.

"My sister was taking a shower. I heard footsteps in the hall outside our door and I was curious, so I quietly opened it and saw Edna. She was trying to open *your* door, Lauren, but you must have locked it when you and your boyfriend went out to dinner. Edna mustn't have had a master key with her because she was tutting away. She did have a couple of fluffy towels with her, so I don't know if you'd asked for some and she was delivering them."

"No, we hadn't," Lauren told her. "Edna had already given us plenty."

"Ha! See, she just wanted an excuse to snoop around while you were out. I think I did you and your boyfriend a favor. Who knows what she might have found in your room?"

"Nothing." Lauren cast her mind back but her conscience was clear. What did Donna think she got up to in her spare time? "Just enough clothes for a weekend away. That's not a crime."

"Hmm." Donna looked disappointed. "Oh, well. She got what was coming to her, anyway. That will teach her to meddle in other people's business and tattle on people."

"But what about Harry, her husband?" Zoe asked. "He seems like a nice man."

"Yes, he does, doesn't he?" Donna agreed. "I'm sure I did him a favor as well. He was probably hen-pecked. Once he gets over the shock of losing her so suddenly, he'll find he can do whatever he wants and have no one to be accountable to. I'm sure he'll learn to love the single life."

Lauren and Zoe glanced at each other. Donna seemed to have totally justified her actions to herself.

"And now, explanation time has come to an end." Donna raised her hand and leveled the gun at their faces.

"But won't your sister wonder where you are?" Lauren asked desperately, her hands tensing on Annie's furry body.

"I told her I had to go into work and cover an urgent shift." Donna laughed. "I pretended I had a text message from the store. She won't be expecting me home for a few hours."

"Oh." Zoe sounded disappointed.

"But wait!" Lauren glanced down at Annie. "You don't want to shoot me while I'm holding Annie. What if you accidentally get Annie, too?"

"Yes, you don't want the death of a totally innocent and gorgeous cat on your conscience – do you?" Zoe added, widening her eyes for an ingenue effect.

"Fine." Donna huffed. "Put the cat down and then I'll shoot you. It *is* a shame in a way – your coffee was excellent and so was your latte art. But I guess you're used to customers telling you that all the time."

"Sometimes," Lauren admitted.

"It's nice to hear," Zoe added. "But what did you really think about Lauren's new raspberry bonus cupcake – the one with the raspberries, strawberries, and blueberries?"

"It *was* really good." Donna nodded. "It's just my luck you're not running a café in Sacramento so I could go there all the time – *except I couldn't even if I wanted to because I can't afford to buy treats like that very often now – because of what Edna did!*" she bellowed.

"Oops." Zoe muttered, glancing at Lauren.

"Yeah." Lauren nodded slightly.

"Time to go, you two. Put the cat down so she doesn't get hurt."

"Brrt?" Annie asked softly, glancing up at Lauren.

Lauren's heart clenched. If she and Zoe didn't come up with a plan fast, she'd never see Annie again.

"I want you to run home when it's safe to do so, and stay there," she whispered into the silver-gray tabby's ear. "Through the private hallway."

"Brrp," Annie murmured, her eyes narrowing slightly.

Lauren didn't know whether her fur baby approved of the hasty plan or not. But it was the best she could think of.

Her gaze fell on the few cupcakes that hadn't sold that day. She'd been able to sneak away for a few minutes at a time and whip up a new batch of raspberry bonuses to serve to the steady stream of customers.

Lauren flicked a glance at Zoe, who caught it, her eyes widening slightly. Zoe tilted her head at the pottery mugs lining the counter.

"Get on with it!" Donna barked. "Put the cat down!"

"I love you." Lauren kissed the top of Annie's head.

"I love you too, Annie." Zoe gave the cat a smile, which Lauren suspected was a trifle forced. "Do what Lauren says."

"Brrt," Annie replied, as if in agreement. She snuggled in Lauren's arms for another second, then hopped down to the ground, between Lauren's feet and the base of the solid counter.

Lauren hoped she had enough time to grab some cupcakes before Donna shot them. Her legs wobbled and her heart thudded.

Squeak! Squeak! Squeak!

"What was that?" Donna looked around, startled, the gun swinging wildly in her hand.

"Justice!" Zoe hurled a pottery mug at Donna's gun hand. It hit her hand but the older woman didn't drop the weapon.

"For Edna and Harry!" Lauren snatched two cupcakes and hurled them at Donna's face.

Zoe threw another pottery mug at Donna's hand. This time it squarely connected.

"Ow!" Donna dropped the revolver. "Ow! You've broken my hand!"

Squeak! Squeak! Squeak!

Zoe took over pelting Donna with cupcakes while Lauren ran around the counter and kicked the gun away.

"Stop!" Donna begged them, sinking onto the floor. "Call an ambulance! Owww. My hand hurts so bad!"

Lauren pulled out her phone and called for the police – and the paramedics – keeping a wary eye on the deadly weapon, now a good distance away from Donna.

"Brrt!" Annie trotted out from behind the counter, dangling a little furry toy in her mouth.

"It's your squeaky mouse." Lauren smiled, proud of her fur baby. "That was a great idea, Annie! Thank you."

"You distracted Donna at just the right time, Annie." Zoe pelted Donna with one last cupcake. "And my pottery efforts have helped save us twice now. Maybe I should continue with it for a bit longer – or even a lot longer. Even if my mugs do have bulges in them." She turned to Lauren. "It's a shame you had to waste those cupcakes on Donna, though. I was thinking we could have them for dessert tonight!"

"Me too," Lauren said ruefully.

"Brrt!"

EPILOGUE

"The gnomes look wonderful. It brings me back to when I was a child and we had them in our garden."

The gray-haired lady gazed out of the window at her rear garden. She sat in a wheelchair in the bright, sunny room, wearing cotton slacks and a blouse in matching violet.

Four gnomes in various spots near the freshly mown lawn seemed to smile at them as they peeked out behind white petaled Morning Glory, golden California Buttercups, and blue California Lilac.

"How can I thank you?" their new friend Iris asked.

"We don't need to be thanked." Zoe grinned.

"It was fun choosing one for you," Lauren added.

"Brrt," Annie agreed.

Lauren would much rather think about the gnomes brightening up Iris's garden than their close call with Donna.

Mitch had arrested Donna, since Detective Castern had been in Sacramento interviewing her sister Barbara, when Lauren made the emergency phone call requesting help.

Donna's broken hand was taken care of at the same time she was arrested. Mitch assured them afterward that she'd made a full confession and would be in jail for a long time.

After the gnomes were delivered, they'd picked up Martha, who directed them to her friend's house. After placing the gnomes in the garden, they'd rung the doorbell, hoping to surprise the elderly lady. It worked.

"You've been so kind to me." Iris sighed. "I don't know what else to say."

"Your pleasure is thanks enough," Mitch said gruffly.

Lauren smiled at him. He was a good one, all right. He'd mowed the small lawn without a second thought, finding the vintage push reel machine in the shed and using it to cut the overgrown grass while she, Annie, Zoe, and Martha debated where to place each gnome.

"Four gnomes isn't as good as the six I had in mind, but it's still pretty good," Martha told her pal.

"You're a great friend, Martha." Iris patted Martha's hand.

"Thanks." Martha beamed. Her gaze collided with Lauren's, Zoe's, Annie's, and Mitch's. "These guys are good friends too – all of them."

"I can see that they are." Iris smiled at all of them. "Thank you – all of you."

"To old friends – and new." Lauren's eyes became the *tiniest* bit misty.

"Brrt!"

The End

I hope you enjoyed reading this mystery. Sign up to my newsletter at **http://www.JintyJames.com** and be among the first to discover when my next book is published! A list of all my titles is on the following page.

TITLES BY JINTY JAMES

Have you read:

Purrs and Peril – A Norwegian Forest Cat Café Cozy Mystery – Book 1

Meow Means Murder – A Norwegian Forest Cat Café Cozy Mystery – Book 2

Whiskers and Warrants – A Norwegian Forest Cat Café Cozy Mystery – Book 3

Two Tailed Trouble – A Norwegian Forest Cat Café Cozy Mystery – Book 4

Paws and Punishment – A Norwegian Forest Cat Café Cozy Mystery – Book 5

Kitty Cats and Crime – A Norwegian Forest Cat Café Cozy Mystery – Book 6

<u>Maddie Goodwell Series (fun witch cozies)</u>

Spells and Spiced Latte - A Coffee Witch Cozy Mystery - Maddie Goodwell 1

Visions and Vanilla Cappuccino - A Coffee Witch Cozy Mystery - Maddie Goodwell 2

Magic and Mocha – A Coffee Witch Cozy Mystery – Maddie Goodwell 3

Enchantments and Espresso – A Coffee Witch Cozy Mystery – Maddie Goodwell 4

Familiars and French Roast - A Coffee Witch Cozy Mystery – Maddie Goodwell 5

Incantations and Iced Coffee – A Coffee Witch Cozy Mystery – Maddie Goodwell 6

Made in United States
North Haven, CT
29 December 2021